THE DRAGON'S OATH

SILVER DRAGON SHIFTER BROTHERS

MARIE JOHNSTON

LE PUBLISHING

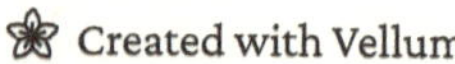 Created with Vellum

Deacon

In hindsight, demanding a human woman swear herself to me in exchange for the life of her father wasn't my best idea. But I saw her and I wanted her, and I need a mate. After shouldering the responsibility of all shifter-kind for so long, I acted selfishly. I know what breaking her word would cost her. Ava is the one who made an oath to me, but I might sacrifice everything to save her from it.

Ava

I'm supposed to hate Deacon, and I shouldn't believe his story about dragon shifters blending in the human world, but the longer I'm around him, the harder it is not to fall under his spell. I humor the oath I made and try to get to know him, but I've got one foot out the door. I've been duped by false promises and handsome faces before, and I'm not giving up everything for a man again. Only Deacon isn't just a man. And he has secrets that could threaten more than my heart.

 va

SITTING this far out in the lake in a boat made it seem like Dad and I were the only people left on earth. No one moved on the shore. The cabins weren't filled with people this early into spring. It'd be closer to Memorial Day when the summer crowd filled narrow beaches and pontoons and Jet Skis littered the lake. In the middle of April, the sun was warm, but the wind had a cool bite. The ice had melted and Dad had planned a two-week camping trip. The timing was perfect as far as I was concerned.

My line dipped, but I knew better than to hope it was a fish. Dad and I used to fish all the time when I was a kid. I'd come home from college and go with him. Then I moved for all the wrong reasons.

There was no good side to Mom's death, but Dad

wasn't afraid to leave for weeks. Nothing was keeping him at home, and he no longer needed to wait until she could get time off of work. So when I showed up on his doorstep, distraught and lost, he did what he did best. He planned a fishing and camping trip.

I let out a sigh. After two weeks of sleeping on a cot in a sleeping bag, I'll be happy to return to my empty life in Minneapolis. I'll have a bed at least—once I find a place to put it.

"Everything okay, kiddo?" Dad adjusted his tan hat. He was dressed like he walked off the pages of a wilderness catalog. Khaki pants, filled with whatever we might need for the afternoon, a long-sleeved plaid shirt, black suspenders, and the hat.

"I'm fine."

"Not the kind of thing a twenty-five-year-old wants to do, huh?"

"No, this is perfect." I had nothing else to do, and I was glad to have someone to be with.

"It's all right. You can tell me. It won't hurt my feelings."

"I'm serious, Dad. I enjoy being with you even if I'm not as passionate about fishing as you are."

Dad grinned and checked his line. "I am passionate about fishing. If I could find a way to make a living doing this, I would. Beats selling insurance any day."

I smiled and tipped my head back to the sun. The heat soaked into my bones while the wind kept me cool. It really was a beautiful day. Boating on a lake in the middle of the Turtle Mountains—nothing could beat it.

Dad still lived in my hometown about an hour away from the Canadian border in North Dakota. But his favorite places to fish were as far north as he could get with no passport. Which was fine with me. I wanted to be with Dad, but I didn't want to be in my hometown where I would be reminded of my poor decisions. And I didn't want to be in Minneapolis. The city had nothing but my best friend, Avril. I certainly didn't have a boyfriend anymore. Or a job.

Broken up with and laid off within forty-eight hours. Wasn't I lucky?

The dark cloud of my ex threatened to darken this gorgeous spring day. No. I would not let anything infringe on the peace and quiet of this lake in the time I got to spend with my dad.

Dad slowly reeled in his line. "I think we need to go a little farther out, where it's deeper."

"You're the expert."

The boat was Dad's baby. He was close to retirement, and he'd been determined to pay it off before then. I didn't touch it. The boat we had growing up wasn't an easy ride, so I never learned to drive it.

"You will be soon. Before the trip is done, I'll teach you."

"Thanks." My spirits perked. I could use a win.

I enjoyed the gentle ruffle of the wind through my hair and leaned back, letting my eyelids drift shut and resting my elbows on the side of the boat. I'd arrived home last Friday. It was Tuesday. Dad and I had been camping for two days, but this was why I came. I was feeling more like myself than I had for years.

The boat jerked and the drone of the engine faded into idle.

I squinted around. "Are we at the magic spot?"

If Dad's goal was to get us right smack in the middle of the big lake, mission accomplished. Green trees in the distance. Gently sloping hills that weren't nearly high enough to be called mountains in the accurately named Turtle Mountains surrounded the water. We were far enough out that I could see the lake cabins that line the shore, but I couldn't look inside their windows and feel like a creeper.

The engine sputtered. I frowned. Dad usually shut the boat down when he found a suitable spot. I glanced over and a cry ripped out of me. The limp form of my dad was slumped sideways, falling between the front seats.

"Dad!" I rushed to his side. The boat rocked as I reached him.

I gripped his shoulders to help him upright. Was this a stroke or heart attack? I had no damn idea. I sold life insurance plans all day; I had nothing to do with the end of actual life itself.

"Help!" Even as I shouted, I knew it was futile. There was no one around, and if they could, they'd still have to call for help and that help would have to get out to me and my dad in time to save him.

"Dad? Can you hear me?"

Shit. His eyes were closed. Was he breathing? I couldn't do a thing with him in the chair. I wrapped my arms around his chest and pulled him to the side and back. He was deadweight.

I strained and pulled. I didn't want to hurt him, but if I couldn't move him so I could drive the boat, it wouldn't matter.

I used every ounce of strength I possessed until I was screaming from the effort. Finally, I made enough progress to lay him out on the floor of the boat.

Maneuvering carefully, I made it around him to the front. He was in a rumpled pile.

A sob escaped, and my vision was blurring. I hoped it was only from tears.

"I'm going to get us back to shore," I croaked. I had no idea how to do that, but the only thing I knew was that I would not idle in this damn thing while I watched my dad die.

~

Deacon

"Did you hear something?" I squinted into the distance. A couple of boats spotted the lake. Nothing but off-season anglers who couldn't wait to get a jump on the sport. I couldn't blame them. I'd rather spend my day in the sun, catching delicious food and enjoying the sun on my scales.

The whole scales thing doesn't happen as often as I'd like, but that was our life. I had a private place by my home where I could shift and soak up the sun.

My brother glanced up from where we were loading patio blocks for Penn's new place into the back of the pickup. The owner of the lake house was on Silver Lake's council and had offered it to us for free if we hauled it. "I thought I heard a shout, but some retiree probably just caught a whopper of a walleye."

I shook my head, my gaze roaming our surroundings.

"Deacon, if someone needs help, they'll shout again."

"No, it's just..." I swept my gaze over the gentle, twinkling blue waves. My sensitive ears picked up the sudden roar of an engine. It sputtered, then jumped to life. I searched for the boat that was making the noise. Didn't take long to find the gleaming white-and-silver fishing boat bouncing erratically over the surface. The engine would roar and then back off until the boat settled down. If the driver kept on the throttle, they might end up vertical.

Steel spotted what I had. "That driver doesn't know what the hell they're doing."

The boat, coupled with the shout I heard earlier, raised an alarm in my brain. "They're in trouble."

"They're gonna be," Steel said sarcastically.

I could get to the boat and pluck the whole thing out of the water and carry it to shore. It was broad daylight, the sun chasing all the shadows away. Wildrose might be part of Silver clan area, but we weren't even open in our natural form there. Humans were a part of our daily life, and we couldn't risk a non-mate knowing about us.

I squinted at the boat, willing my eyesight to be as keen as my hearing. There was only one figure on the boat. My vision was acute enough to see the person's hair that glowed like spun gold whipping around her head.

"Female," I murmured in a reverent tone.

Steel glanced at me from the corner of his eye. As I watched her frantic pace across the water, I yearned to make out more details. Was she short or tall? What color were her eyes? Did she have a pleasing scent?

The boat lurched, and I snapped back to reality.

"She's going to crash the damn thing." I jumped in the driver's seat and shouted to my brother, "You getting in or what?"

Steel clamored into the passenger seat. "You know I'm always up for adventure."

I punched the pickup into gear and pulled out of the gas station. A road curved around the entire lake, serving all the cabins and permanent residents lining the shore. I raced in the direction the boat was heading.

Was she going to slow down? It didn't look like it.

Steel pointed out his window. "If she doesn't drown herself, she's going to come to an abrupt stop at that two-story red cabin."

I willed that place to be a vacation lake home. This time of year the lake was quiet, the vacationers minimal. There were still some people who lived in their cabins year-round and braved the snow dumps every winter.

That snow had melted and there was nothing but rocks for the boat to crash into.

Slow the hell down. You're going to die before I can even see the face that goes with that beautiful hair.

Dragons were suckers for anything that resembled gems and precious metals.

I bypassed the driveway and drove around the house, weaving to miss a firepit and swing set, until I got as close to the boat dock as possible. The boater wasn't going to make the dock, but she shouldn't hit far away.

By some miracle, the human managed to slow the boat down before it hit the rocks. The screech of the hull against the stone made my sensitive ears ache. Steel winced and shook his head.

The woman was knocked down. Her cry reached my ears and lit a fire deep in my belly. I slammed the pickup in park and jumped out. Leaving the door open, I charged toward the boat.

"H-help!" The woman didn't jump up and down and wave her arms, nor did she scramble out of the boat to look for someone. She dropped at an odd angle to her knees and bent until I almost couldn't see her.

I reached the boat. An older man was sprawled out on

the bottom. There was barely enough room for her to straddle him. She was pumping his chest. CPR. I inhaled and inspected each smell that flowed into me.

She was an adult, but young. Traces of her scent were similar to the male. Her father. But he was dying. I could barely hear the flutter of his heart, a mere quiver. His brain and body were growing more and more oxygen deprived.

His situation was dire, but I could help. On rare occasions, it was allowed, and this was one such time.

My brother's muffled footsteps on the greening grass barely resonated in my awareness. My attention was back on the woman. I still couldn't get a good look at her face, but it didn't matter. I knew one unequivocal thing about her.

She was mine.

va

I OPENED my mouth to yell for help again, but snapped it shut. I didn't stop chest compressions. The last CPR course I took was eight years ago when I wanted to babysit Tina Feliz instead of working at the local diner for my part-time job.

A man stood by the side of the boat. If I wasn't so desperate to save my dad, I'd probably pass out from the powerful impact of his sheer masculine beauty.

As it was, I didn't care. "Can you call 9-1-1? My dad collapsed."

Another man rounded the boat. He was almost as magnificent as the first guy. Again, I only cared if their stunning looks gave them more ability to save Dad.

Neither man had a phone in their hand or was moving like they were going to find some assistance.

"Call for help," I snapped. My arms were fatiguing. I was at an awkward angle. I couldn't get much leverage and my lungs were burning. How long would it take an ambulance to arrive? What if it was on me alone to save my dad?

I lost my boyfriend and my job within days of each other. My mom died a couple of years ago. I couldn't lose Dad too.

"I can help your father." The first man's voice was rich. I was tempted to close my eyes and wallow in the deep timbre, but I continued chest compressions for whatever it was worth. "But I need your oath."

The second man whipped his head toward the first, his eyes wide. When he directed his gaze back toward me, disbelief and pity mingled in his gunmetal-gray eyes.

"Whatever, call 9-1-1." My compressions were losing steam, growing erratic, and lacking in force. My shoulders and back muscles were screaming. This was the most I'd done for working out in a long time.

The first man, the one who wanted an oath of some sort, inclined his head to the other side of the boat. The second guy ran around. I yelled as the two of them grabbed the sides and hauled the boat halfway onto shore.

"Grab her father," the first guy said.

"No, you need to call for help first."

Ignoring me, the first man put a brawny leg inside the boat and wrapped his powerful arms around me. He lifted me like I was little more than a stray dog. The band of his arms was so tight I could barely breathe. I opened my mouth to scream for help, but he clamped a hand over my lips.

His deep growl reverberated in my ear. "You're not

going to scream. You're going to save your father by promising yourself to me."

I trembled as I watched the second man carefully lay my father out on the grass. His gaze lifted to the man imprisoning me before he steadily continued compressions, his lips in a flat line.

"I swear I can save your father's life," the first man repeated. "Now it's your turn."

Heat radiated into me as if I was standing against ten heat lamps. His hold was firm. I couldn't move. I could try to scream again, only it was disturbing that I didn't want to.

"I'll explain everything later, but you're running out of time, Goldie."

Who the hell was Goldie? I shook my head.

"You have less than a minute before nothing will bring your father back from the dead."

Dad's limp form rocked with each compression. The disturbing crackle of his ribs made me nauseous. But the deep sense that this man was telling the truth about my father's impending death made me give a shaky nod. The man turned his nose into my hair, his lips brushing the shell of my ear. "Swear yourself to me."

Little did he know I'd just been thrown away. If this would somehow save my dad, I would go with it. "I swear myself to you." My voice trembled.

He eased his hold off of me rather than a sudden release that would send me reeling. I wanted to wipe the smugly satisfied look off his face. His sapphire-blue gaze captivated me for a fraction of a second before he turned his back on me and crossed to my father.

Kneeling at Dad's head, he held his hands out. The

second guy sat back on his heels and rested his hands on his thighs.

I hugged myself as I watched what was happening. As far as I could tell, there was a whole lot of nothing.

I detected a low humming. Which of the two men was carrying a tune while my dad's heart gave out?

Dad's eyes remained closed, but a grunt escaped from his lips and his back arched. His mouth twisted open in a silent yell and the sickening sound of crunching bones resumed.

I lunged for Dad. The second man intercepted me, his hands gripping my shoulders. "That's the healing."

I strained against him. He was as strong as the first man.

"W-what's he doing?"

"Just what he swore he would," the man said, his tone gruff. "He'll finish in a moment. Your father will remain unconscious, but he'll be alive, and we'll transport him to the hospital."

The guy by my father's head rose, straightening to his towering height. His gaze caressed me, soft as a feather, but when he spoke it was to the other man. "I'll carry him to the pickup and take them to the hospital. Can you deal with the boat?"

The second guy dipped his head. "I'll call Penn." With their full attention off me, I rushed to Dad's side. The pallor was gone. A healthy flush colored his skin. I sank to my knees and felt his neck for a pulse.

Strong hands landed on my shoulders, and a wave of heat swept over me as the man I swore an oath to crouched behind me. "He's alive and recovering," he said more gently than I expected. "We will tell the hospital that he collapsed. His ribs are mended, and the blockage in his heart is gone. They won't be able to explain to you what happened, and you will only cause problems if you insist they keep looking."

The hint of threat in his tone made me jerk away from him as I leaped to my feet. "Don't touch me."

He stepped forward, and I had nowhere to go without stepping on Dad. "You asked for help and you'll have to pay the price. You swore an oath to be mine."

Just as abruptly, he nudged me out of his way and stooped to gather Dad into his arms. With ease, he adjusted Dad across his shoulders in a firefighter's carry. The man made an unconscious adult seem as light as an inflatable doll.

"He passed out. That's what you'll tell them." He gave me one last intent look before he started up the incline toward a yard that had a black pickup parked in the middle.

I followed him, only because he had Dad. Oath be damned. Others had made promises to me and broke them. They're nothing but words.

DEACON

I LAID the woman's father across the back seat and tucked his legs inside before I shut the door. She glared at me and climbed into the passenger seat. I suppressed a grin as I turned to Steel. His grave gaze was unsettling. My younger brother wasn't one to be hung up on things like tradition and rules, but he wasn't hiding his disapproval of what I did.

"She calls to me," was all I said.

"You made a *human* swear an oath. She knows nothing of what that means." Steel's gaze filled with sympathy as he glanced at the golden-haired woman in the passenger seat. Her impatience was like a beacon that my inner beast wanted to answer immediately. He didn't like to leave her waiting. The feeling told me that what I did was not a mistake.

"She'll learn. It'll be fine." Eventually. Steel hit on the major concern. She was human. And she swore an oath to a dragon shifter.

"Will she be fine when Venus learns of this?"

I wanted to groan every time I thought of Venus. She'd been a part of my life basically since I was born. "I'll deal with Venus."

"Yeah." He snickered. "You do that. Get going. I need to call Penn and clean this mess up."

I hated dragging my youngest brother into this mess, but as a Silver, he needed to know what was going on. I wasn't as concerned about Venus Jade as I was about her family.

But I couldn't think of that now. I had a more important task ahead of me.

I crawled into the driver's seat and was immediately hit with her cherry almond scent. It curled around me like a welcoming blanket. My blood heated and I could easily imagine sinking my teeth into her creamy flesh.

I had gotten to see her eyes earlier. A blue-green color that was as soft as her ripe curves. My human was lovely.

I started the engine. The sooner they cared for her father, the sooner she would realize I had saved the man. Then she'd have to live up to her oath.

She peered into the back seat long enough to make

sure her father was still alive. I could hear his steady breathing better than she could see the rise and fall of his chest.

"He's going to be unconscious for a solid twenty-four hours," I told her.

"How can you predict that?"

I wanted to groan, her melodious voice stroked my eardrums. Perhaps it was best she didn't know her effect on me. "It's not something we do often, but my kind has healed enough humans to know that near death takes a while to come back from."

I reached across her to snag the seat belt. Her innate sweet smell bloomed with the spike in her heart rate. I'd always had a sweet tooth.

"What are you doing?" Her voice was strangled. I buckled her seat belt, and she snapped, "I could have done that myself."

"But you didn't." I backed out and got on the road. "What's your name?"

She glanced in the back seat again. If I hadn't buckled her, she'd have probably turned around and shoved her round ass in the air so she could keep her eye on her dad the whole time. I had cost myself quite the view.

"Ava."

It suited her. "Ava what?"

She didn't reply, just stared militantly out the windshield.

This wouldn't do. I slowed to a stop to keep her father from rolling onto the floorboard. I leaned over the console, as close to her as I was when I grabbed the seat belt. She shrank against the door.

"You swore an oath to me, Ava." My tone was serious, as grave as the situation she didn't know she was in. "I'm aware you don't realize what that means, but I'm going to hold you to it. I saved your father's life. I healed his heart, I mended his broken bones, and I repaired the damage lack of oxygen did to his brain. In return, you're going to be my mate—my wife. You're going to live here. Your life is now with me."

Her eyes widened with each sentence. The blues and greens in her irises mixed like emeralds and sapphires melting together. I could get lost in them.

"I'm not going to be your—"

"I can undo all the healing." I wouldn't, but it was the best card I had to play. Dirty, but necessary. She wouldn't call my bluff. She couldn't—or we'd both suffer.

Her lips formed a troubled line. "How did you heal him?"

It was a sign of how scared she was for her father that she only thought to ask now how I did it. "Some of us are able to share our healing ability. For your father, his condition was dire, but it wasn't complicated for my kind."

"Your what?"

I hit the gas again and took us to the highway that led to Wildrose. "Listen, what I say is going to make you think I'm crazy, but listen with an open mind and when you doubt what I say, remember what happened with your father."

"Okay?"

Good enough. "We are the species that inhabit this area. We are from a long line of shifters. Magical shifters."

"Magical shifters? As opposed to Muggles?" Her slight sarcastic tone made a smile twitch my lips.

"Shifting is as natural to me as breathing. The same

with being able to heal people. To me, it's like going for a run, but to you, it seems like magic."

She leveled her stare at me. Direct. I liked it. "Look, I can't deny that my dad wasn't breathing before you showed up, and now he is. But I don't see how you think that makes me your wife."

We were almost at Wildrose. It was a small enough community that the hospital was only minutes away. I didn't have time to tell her about the history of my people. "We'll get there, but you have to believe me."

"Or you'll undo all the healing?" Animosity infused her words.

"That too." I couldn't say it with much inflection. I only hurt others when necessary, and it was usually for the protection of others. I couldn't magically stop her dad's heart, nor could I withdraw my energy. She just really needed not to know that right now.

She crossed her arms under her breasts, angling her body away from me, and glowered out the window.

The beast inside of me hated I upset her. I tried to tell myself it was necessary, but that didn't help. I pulled into a spot in the hospital parking lot. Before she could undo her seat belt, I put my hand on hers.

When those brilliant eyes of hers met mine, I said, "Look, I'm not going to hurt your dad. I can't undo anything, and the oath is going to be hard enough on you as it is. I'll do everything I can to keep your father hale and hearty."

"You were bluffing?"

I nodded, clenching my jaw. She caught me in a lie. Would that do more damage to my efforts than help them?

She softened under my touch. I knew she didn't believe me about the oath, but I made progress.

I lifted her father out of the pickup and she went through the process of admitting him into the small Wildrose ER. When her father was rolled into an exam room and she rushed behind him, I realized she hadn't asked for my name.

~

AVA

I PERCHED on the chair next to my father's bed in a tiny ER room. The staff hadn't changed him out of his clothing. His blood pressure was better than it'd been for twenty years, and he had the pulse of a collegiate athlete.

That man had indeed healed him.

Most of the staff didn't seem to know my dad's savior, but there were a few who greeted him with bright smiles. Especially the attractive women.

That was not jealousy heating my blood.

The curious looks those women shot my way were unnerving. I grew up in a smaller community, but not with a population as small as Wildrose. I wouldn't know if someone was new to my hometown. But I didn't think I would look at them as if they had won the lottery and a dream vacation on the same night.

The triage nurse called the man who saved Dad by what must be his name. Deacon. An unusual name for an unusual man.

The doctor that met with me about Dad eyed Deacon like he was the last crispy slice of bacon on the plate. The burn in my gut was not new, and I hated it. I disliked the man for it. I'd had enough of jealousy when I was with Chance. Deacon acted like he didn't notice the extra attention the women in this clinic gave him, but Chance had pretended to be clueless like that at first too.

It didn't matter what state I was in, or what town, men were all the same. I'd call them animals, but I'd seen tomcats with more faithfulness than Chance.

The nurse attending Dad swept into the room on a cloud of patchouli. Her long black hair was in a braid and the no-nonsense creases around her eyes told me she'd likely been in the medical field for several years. "Dr. Soto would like to admit your dad until he regains consciousness."

I nodded, grateful that neither of us would be kicked to the curb. I couldn't pick up and carry Dad as easily as Deacon.

As if thinking about the big man summoned him, he sauntered in. I snapped my gaze away from him, back to my father like I was trying to remind myself what was really important when all I really wanted to do was get lost in those sapphire-blue eyes and imagine what it would be like if he threw me around like he did Dad.

I crossed one leg over another, too aware of how suddenly sensitive I was between my thighs. "Do you know how long that will be?"

I wasn't looking at Deacon, but heat licked my body. Was he watching me?

"No. His breathing is fine; the rest of his vitals are fine. We just want to make sure that he remains stable until he regains consciousness. If he doesn't come to soon, the doctor will transfer him." She shuffled several papers. "I need you to sign these while I take another set of vitals."

I ignored Deacon the entire time I went through the paperwork. Why was he still here? The nurse prepped my dad for transport to a regular room.

A young man entered, wearing the same maroon scrubs as the nurse, but his name tag read CNA.

"Will you help me get him into a hospital gown?" the nurse said to the CNA. She patted my shoulder. "While we change your dad, you can wait right outside. I'll let you know when we're done."

I soaked in as much of her kind tone as possible. Ever since Dad collapsed, my universe had been spinning out of control and I didn't know what was up or down. But I did as she asked and waited in the hall.

Deacon leaned his large body against the wall beside me. "You're staying with me tonight."

Startled, I met his deep-blue gaze. "I will do no such thing," I hissed. "I'm staying here, with him." I wasn't even thinking about that wife shit right now. It was hard enough to think about anything with him standing so close.

"Your father's fine, and there's nowhere to sleep."

I kept my voice at a whisper. It was better than his deep rumble that I swore everyone in the bustling ER could hear. "I'm sure there's a chair in his room. That'll be fine."

His lips pressed together, and his nostrils flared. I briefly wondered if he was smelling me, but I realized that would be ridiculous. If I thought about him smelling me, then I thought about him eating me and that led to a dangerous place. A place where my breasts grew heavy and achy and I wondered how his big hands would feel closed over them.

He groaned and abruptly spun toward the wall. "I

don't know where your thoughts are going, Ava, but you're killing me."

I stifled a gasp. My cheeks burned. There was no way he could know what I was thinking. No way.

"I'm staying with my dad tonight," I reiterated, more to reorient myself.

"Then I'll be here too."

The audacity of this man. How did I go from a boyfriend who couldn't wait to get away from me to a giant of a man that I couldn't shake? "Where? And how? You're not family."

He placed an arm on the wall above my head, his body curving over mine. His smoldering pine scent boxed me in. "I take the health of my father-in-law seriously because it affects my mate."

This was the second time he said mate. I didn't know what kind of town Wildrose was. It was only an hour north of where I'd grown up. Maybe they talked differently. But when he said that word, it conjured images I didn't need to be thinking. I didn't need to consider what it was like to mate with him.

Wariness overtook my consternation. The big sexy man was irritating me, but it'd been a long day. Dad and I had gotten up early to get the best fishing hours. Then I had thought I lost him. And now he was unconscious in the next room and the best-looking guy I'd ever met was telling me I was his mate.

I sagged against the wall. "Can you give me some space?"

Concern etched into his features. I wasn't prepared for that. I'd seen a range of emotions on this man—arrogance, anger, calm. Mostly directed at me. I wouldn't be able to weather attention from a man like this on a good day, but the adrenaline that had been propping me up was draining away. I was tired.

"What's wrong, Ava?"

He seemed to enjoy saying my name. I never thought it fit me. Other than being short and simple, it wasn't plain enough. Those three letters arranged to make two beautiful syllables. Nothing about me arranged into a beautiful anything. I was neither tall nor short. I wasn't skinny, but I wasn't plus size. My hair wasn't brown, but it wasn't blonde. My eyes weren't blue, but they also weren't green.

Ordinarily, I'd brush off the attention of a guy like this. It wasn't real. How many times in college, before Chance, had a hot guy acted like a wingman? He'd distract me so his buddy could snag my prettier friend? Then Chance had shown actual interest, and I'd been hooked harder than the trout Dad caught yesterday.

When would Deacon show his true intentions? He'd find someone sexier, more educated, like that doctor from earlier, and he'd be gone before I could tell myself guys like him didn't go for women like me. It hurt when Chance had done it last week and I'd been with him for three years. For some reason, the sting Deacon would leave behind seemed worse.

I scrubbed a hand over my face. "I'm exhausted." For so many reasons.

He pushed away from the wall, taking the wall of heat with him, and left me in the enclave outside of Dad's room. He was back in a second, rolling a chair across the floor.

He didn't have to tell me to sit before I sank down and propped my elbows on my knees. I put my head in my hands and blocked out the world. I couldn't seem to block him out, but his wall of heat was back, soothing my aching muscles and calming the pounding at my temples.

We didn't talk. He waited with me. What would the situation with Dad have been like without him?

I didn't want to think that Dad would be dead, but when I crashed that boat he had been gone. I thought he was gone as soon as he slumped over. Panic welled at the memory. It had been hopeless. We'd been in the middle of a damn lake. I crashed the boat. The ambulance wouldn't have made it in time.

And there was Deacon. In that window where Dad could be saved, Deacon had... what?

Healed him. It was indisputable. Dad was unconscious, but he was still with me. And I was going to find out what it had cost me.

THREE

AVA WAS STUBBORN, I'd give her that. She'd turned the chair sideways in order to curl against the wall while she dozed. Her sleep was light and restless. It'd have to be sleeping like that. I repressed the urge to gather her into my arms and curl her onto my lap so she could snooze against my chest. I would endure the discomfort of the chair instead. But she wasn't ready for that yet.

And my kind at the clinic were already asking too many questions. Dr. Soto was wondering why I was rebuffing her advances and hovering over a human. I didn't live in Wildrose, but I came here enough—for work and for play. The shifters here knew who I was. They also knew that this human woman was not Venus.

Would my brothers and I be able to keep on top of the rumors before they made their way to Jade Hills and the female I was supposed to mate with at the end of next week? I didn't know, but I couldn't bring myself to leave the hospital and deal with it. Ava was my priority. I also couldn't make calls and risk being overheard by the humans who worked in the hospital.

Steel would've told Penn what I'd done. The council might hunt them down for an explanation while I was stuck here. I circled around the nurses' station and ended up back in the room of Dorian Payne. I assumed Ava's last name was also Payne. There was no ring on her finger, no indent that she had worn one long term.

I wanted my ring on her finger. I knew which one I'd pick. A princess-cut ruby with a silver setting.

Ava shifted in her chair and readjusted her head. One of the aides had given her a blanket and a pillow. The pillow was slipping backward. I nudged it forward and Ava murmured as she sought to find a modicum of comfort.

She sighed and gave up. Straightening, she stretched her back and rotated her head from side to side. Then she gathered her blankets and the pillow and stood. As she flipped around the chair, she spotted me and jumped. "Good Lord, you're still here."

I frowned. "Where else would I be?"

She hugged her bedding to herself and sat back in the chair. "Your home. Don't you live here?"

"I live in Silver Lake. It's about twenty minutes away, and I'm not leaving here without you."

Irritation deepened her scowl. She spread the blanket over her lap and stuffed the pillow between her shoulder and the wall. "So why am I supposed to be your wife?"

Fatigue had worn her down. From the way she acted around the staff, I got the impression she was timid, that she didn't speak her mind. But around me, she was bolder. Cranky. I wasn't used to cranky females.

I wasn't worried about Dorian overhearing what I was going to tell her, but I ensured the door was shut. I stood across from her, my shoulder against the wall. "My name's Deacon Silver. I'm the leader of the Silver clan."

Confusion turned her mouth down. "You mean a tribe?"

My people lived in the Turtle Mountains, adjacent to the reservation and among the Chippewa and Metis. "Indigenous tribes are completely different from our clans. The tribes are comprised of humans." I tapped my chest. "I am a shifter. A dragon shifter."

She giggled. Not the reaction I expected. I stuffed my hands into my pockets.

Her eyes narrowed on me, and her smile faded. "You really believe that?"

"I wouldn't have been able to heal your father if I wasn't a dragon shifter." If I wasn't who I was in my clan.

Her gaze strayed to her dad. As she thought about what I said, she licked her lower lip. It had been unmistakable. Her father had been on death's doorstep, and now he wasn't. She wanted to claim I was crazy, but she'd seen a miracle she couldn't deny.

"So, say you're a dragon shifter. What does that mean?"

The room was dark. The only light was streaming from under the door and through the windows from the parking lot lights, but I could describe the exact shade of the pink of her tongue. A detail I would keep to myself. That would definitely shock her. "It means we've been here through the dawn of time. And to be here longer, we made some concessions before humans littered the face of the planet." I winced. "Sorry, I don't hate humans, but we don't talk about our history around them."

"Humans are pests?" Her annoyed tone only conveyed her crankiness.

Dumping new and strange information on her would not help her disposition. I crooked my fingers. "Stand up."

She burrowed into her pillow like she was shrinking away from me. "Why?"

"Because you're tired and crabby and you need to get some decent rest."

Her glare didn't diminish with my explanation. "I told you, I'm not leaving my dad."

"I'm not asking you to." I held my hand out, hoping she'd take it so I didn't have to lift her out of her chair. The last thing I wanted was to have her holler at me and bring the nurses running.

"Then what are you asking me to do?"

I couldn't believe she swore herself to me so readily when she seemed to have a personality that wanted to question me every step of the way. Growing up, knowing I was next in line to lead Silver clan and our people, I wasn't accustomed to her attitude. A general attitude from humans, yes. But she wasn't just any human. She was mine.

"I am a hell of a lot more comfortable than that chair."

Her eyes flared, and she shook her head. "No, no, no. I'm not sitting on you. I'm not *sleeping* on you."

I nearly rolled my eyes, something I hadn't done since I was a teenager decades ago. I was a hell of a lot better than that chair. But I used the only thing that got her to agree before. "You don't want your dad to wake up and feel like crap because he scared you so much you crashed the boat and spent the night in the hospital, getting no sleep, do you?"

Her lips pressed into a line. They were a paler pink than her tongue, but overall, she seemed wan. She was tired and since I'd first met her hours ago, she had eaten nothing. Finally, she rose.

I took the pillow and tossed it on the foot of the bed. Her father didn't twitch. It took a lot of energy to heal from a near-death experience, even if I loaned him much of mine to do the initial mending.

I sat and took her hand. She tried to snatch it away, but I drew her to me. "Come on," I coaxed, never having had to talk a woman onto my lap before.

It was like her knees gave out. She was tense, like it made her grumpier that she had relented. Before she talked herself out of standing up and finding another chair, I cradled her to me and laid her head on my shoulder. "Get some rest."

"You're really bossy." She was asleep in a minute.

Only after her breathing grew even and her body melted into mine did I let the awareness of her scent and her curves sink in.

Cherry almond imprinted itself over my olfactory nerves. Her body was warm, but not as warm as mine. I had an arm around her back and another anchoring her legs over my lap. Her soft breath puffed against my shirt. She felt right. But I couldn't let myself think about getting lost in her body, or she'd wake up and get more irritable from the giant erection pressed against her hip. So I contented myself with holding my new mate.

～

AVA

I'D NEVER BEEN SO warm and cozy. My bed was a little hard, and there was a kink in the left side of my neck, but I didn't want to move. Heat seeped into me. I'd never need another blanket in my life if I stayed here, just like this.

A deep rumble came from within my bed. "Your father is going to wake up soon."

I whined and burrowed deeper into my flannel sheets.

Wait. I didn't have flannel sheets.

Oh, I was camping with Dad. But my sleeping bag wasn't flannel either.

Memories rushed back and ended with Deacon gathering me onto his lap. As much as I had wanted to fight him, I succumbed to overwhelming fatigue. Since I didn't remember waking up and getting off him, that must mean—

My eyes flew open, and I scrambled off him. My stiff body protested. I groaned.

He rose behind me and put his hands at my waist. "Are you all right?"

I tried to spin away from him, but his grip was firm, unyielding. And I liked it.

I stepped away, putting distance between us. Cooler air rushed around me and I instantly missed his heat. "I'm fine," I mumbled.

He reluctantly withdrew his hands. "Your father will wake up soon and you need to be prepared with what you're going to tell him."

"What do you mean? I'm going to tell him the truth."

He kept his steady gaze on me until I started to squirm. Right. The truth. The shifter thing. I didn't bother claiming there was no such thing. I'd grown up learning about the beliefs of the ancestors of people in the area. Scandinavian folktales. Native American legends. Devils Lake, the lake my hometown was named after was originally supposed to mean spirit water, but I'd heard a few stories about how the lake was named while growing up.

None of the stories I heard included dragons, but I was too worn out to argue, and Deacon clearly bought into every word he said. It'd be pointless to say otherwise. "What am I supposed to say again?"

"That you met me after he collapsed, we had an instant connection, and you're going to stay in Silver Lake with me."

He made it sound too easy. Too easy not to return to Devils Lake with Dad. Too easy not to go back to the city and look for another job. Too easy to stay with Deacon and follow this connection to wherever it would lead.

I was done taking the easy road. "That doesn't work for me."

He arched a dark brow. The fluorescent light made the caramel highlights glint in his hair as much as it did outside. Was his mahogany shade natural? Never mind. I couldn't be obsessing about his hair at a time like this.

"I'll tell him…" I pressed my fingers to my temples.

The pounding was returning. I could go for a solid breakfast and some water. I glanced at the clock on the wall. It was midmorning. I had slept on a strange man for hours. In a hospital room.

How many people had come in through the night to check on Dad only to see me snuggled with a man I'd just met? They didn't know I'd just met him, but I did.

What happened to my life?

Wasn't that a question I'd been asking myself since before Chance dumped me?

Deacon reached behind him and rolled a hospital tray in front of me. He lifted off the thick gray cover to reveal two slices of toast, scrambled eggs, a bowl of oatmeal, two slices of bacon, orange juice, and tiny packets of peanut butter and jelly.

"That's a lot of food." I had been in the hospital for two days when I'd gotten my appendix out as a teenager. I knew what hospital food tasted like. But my stomach rumbled, wanting every tasteless morsel of that food in my belly.

"It should still be warm. I wanted to make sure you had something when you woke up." He tilted his head toward Dad. "They'll bring more when he wakes up."

I was tempted to calculate the cost. The story of my life. But Dad's insurance should cover a couple of meals. I took a seat in the chair that was still warm from Deacon's body heat. If I was less hungry and more stubborn, I'd stand to eat.

I didn't bother to slather anything on the toast. I shoved a corner into my mouth. Satisfaction entered Deacon's eyes as he watched me.

"Did you eat?" I asked around my mouthful of bread.

He didn't take his eyes off my mouth. "We'll get a proper meal when we leave."

I swallowed and shoved the other half of the piece of toast in my mouth. I would be more self-conscious of the way he stared if I wasn't so hungry. I methodically worked my way through everything on the tray. When I was full, I pushed the tray away.

The manners my mom taught me made me say, "Thanks." I even managed to sound appreciative.

"You have a hearty appetite. That's good."

The food turned into lead. "I haven't eaten since yesterday morning."

His lips formed a troubled line. "What did I say to offend you?"

"Nothing."

He folded his arms across his broad chest and it made his biceps bulge bigger. "It's not nothing. Tell me so I don't do it again."

If he had said anything else, I probably would've kept my mouth shut. But he acted disturbed that he insulted me. He offered to change his behavior. I'd never gotten as much from Chance. "My ex used to comment on how much I eat. You know, the stereotypical stuff most women get."

The muscles on each side of his jaw flexed. "I'm familiar with how human women have been made to feel about their size. Rest assured, I won't make you feel that way."

And that brought up the whole shifter thing and how he expected me to lie to my dad. Not only that, he expected me to stay in another town with him. "So the dragon shifter thing."

His gaze strayed to the door, like he was worried someone would overhear.

"It's a secret? Is it just you or what?"

"If you're asking if there are other dragons around, yes. But we blend with humans. We live among humans. Act like them. No one knows we're different unless you become part of our community through mating."

"What's the point of that?"

"Your kind hasn't historically reacted the best to new things they find scary." He lifted his hands with his shrug. "With the standards of today? I don't think we'd face a mob of pitchforks, but we're also not crazy about facing a mob full of cameras and live feeds."

My lips twitched at the humorous image. "So you stay secret for safety reasons?"

"Yes, and because it's meant to be that way. It was a trade our people made eons ago. It's this or die out."

"You hide?" I didn't miss the tightening of his mouth.

"No. We blend. We have rules about shifting and our behavior. Wildrose is more mixed with humans than Silver Lake, but we congregate in communities of our own clan. It keeps conflict to a minimum. We have schools for our young. They grow up and get jobs that help our communities run. They pay taxes. We're our own people, but we live as humans when we can."

I thought about what he said. Have I ever driven through a shifter community? There were a lot of small towns in the state and across the border in Canada. "Who's in charge?"

"I am."

I waited for him to elaborate. He didn't. "Of your community? Or is it clan?"

"I am the oldest Silver in the Silver clan, so I'm in charge of all shifters."

He spoke with such assuredness and authority that a warm flush stole across my body. The walls of the hospital room closed in, and I nearly forgot that we weren't alone until I heard a groan.

I gasped. My chair clattered against the wall as I darted to his side. "Dad, Dad? Are you okay? How are you feeling?"

His eyelids fluttered open, but he looked around the room while he blinked and stretched. "Where am I? What happened?" He glanced at the IV in his left arm to the blood pressure cuff around his right bicep. "Am I in the hospital?" He peered at me with groggy blue eyes then his gaze darted to Deacon. "Who are you?"

He was trying to sit up, but I gently pressed on his shoulders. "Let me get the nurse and then I'll tell you everything that happened."

CHAPTER
FOUR

D eacon

OVERALL, Dorian took Ava's story in stride. The hospital made it believable, but he was confused about why he passed out. Dr. Soto mentioned the possibilities of heat stroke or exhaustion and shrugged off the rest. Ava practically vibrated with the need to tell him he had a heart attack and had been as close to death as a human could get, but she didn't.

Dorian had eaten his meal with as much gusto as his daughter. He maneuvered the hospital tray to the side of the bed. "I hope they're ready with those discharge papers any minute now. I hate hospitals."

He and Ava exchanged glances. There was a story there, and I wasn't used to being the one without the information.

Silver Lake, where the majority of my people lived,

was smaller than Wildrose. I knew people's stories. I knew their parents and their grandparents and had heard all the rumors. But I knew very little about Ava.

"Um, Deacon's brother dealt with the boat. I ruined it, I'm so sorry. I think our time fishing is done." She refused to look at me. "I know we have over a week left on our trip, but we can pack up camp and go to a motel or something. Maybe shore fish? I'm so sorry."

"Oh, honey. I'm the one who's sorry. I've been working overtime to pay for that damn boat before I retire. I guess this is the world's way of showing me I don't need it. We can go home."

I cut off my low growl before it did more than make Ava and her father look around. Like hell she was leaving. "Ava, didn't you mention staying with your dad?"

Her expression hardened. "I took a vacation to be with my father, and I was afraid I lost him. He should be at home. *Resting.*" She didn't drop her hard stare.

Stubborn woman.

Dorian patted her hand, his eyes crinkling at the corners. He seemed like a kind man. He'd probably been a good father, like mine had been. "I'm sure after the scare I gave you, you want to leave as soon as possible. But I feel great. Wow, what a long night of sleep can do."

This time, Ava peeked at me. Her eyes widened when her father asked, "Does Wildrose have a motel?"

I fought a grin while her shoulders went rigid. "We don't need to stay."

Ava might hate me more, but someday she'd realize I was fighting for her. "My brother said he rescued all your fishing stuff. There's still some good shore fishing around here."

Dorian's expression brightened. "Oh, and we can still

camp. We can sleep in our tents. That's fine with you, isn't it, Ava?"

"Oh—okay. Tent camping it is."

I almost growled again. Ava wasn't taking her oath seriously. I didn't want her slipping out of my grasp, but I didn't want to take her away from her father. I hadn't had enough time with mine. There were moments when I missed him so acutely it was like a physical stab between my ribs.

So I went with the first idea that sprang into my mind. "How about I join you?"

They were both surprised, but dismay darkened Ava's features.

I kept going, the idea snowballing. She thought she was being clever, but I could be crafty. "I can show you around. In fact, there's a little-known spot that has a killer walleye and bass population."

I hooked her father completely.

Ava's pink lips pressed into a militant line. "Don't you have a job or something that we'd be taking you away from?"

"It's flexible. Steel owes me some vacation days anyway." He could cover for me. He'd need to. I gave her a grin that must look like I was ready to devour her down to the bone. It'd been a long several hours with her lush little ass resting on my thighs all night.

A flush spread across her cheeks.

Her father clinched the deal. "I'd sure appreciate it. And it's probably good to have another set of eyes in case I collapse again." He patted Ava's hand. "I don't want to worry you again."

Her sigh was so faint that I was probably the only one to hear it. My chest swelled with triumph.

"You'll need your own tent and food supplies," she said as if that was going to deter me.

"Not an issue at all." My grin hadn't faded and her stare sharpened. "You have no idea how much I'm looking forward to it."

~

AVA

DEACON DROPPED me and Dad off by Dad's pickup. It was parked by the boat dock with the boat trailer still attached like a slap in the face. I took Dad's keys and stomped to the vehicle to start it. Dad stayed behind to give Deacon directions to our campsite.

I couldn't believe that man wormed his way into the rest of my week. He was intent on making me fulfill that silly promise.

What if I have to stay? What if to protect Dad from the anxiety of Deacon's crazy claims I have to do what I supposedly promised? What if I have to do this weird dating thing with a man I just met? Wasn't that what Tinder was for? Only I was free to leave after a Tinder date. At least that was what I'd heard.

I should've hit dating apps instead of settling for Chance.

Dad climbed into the passenger seat. "He seems like a nice kid."

I laughed, mostly to release some nervous energy. "He can be pushy."

"I'm so glad he was there to help you." Moisture glittered in his eyes. "I never want to leave you in a bad position like that again."

"It's not like you meant to, Dad."

I pulled out of the parking lot and followed the winding roads around the lake to where our tent was set up. Dad kept glancing at me, but I waited for him to speak when he was ready.

It wasn't long. "He seems quite taken with you."

Dad went from almost dying on me in the middle of the lake to telling me he thought a boy liked me. That was so Dad.

"Oh?"

"I know you're probably not looking. I don't blame you after your deal with—" He waved his hand around as if saying my ex's name might conjure him. "But I don't want you to miss the forest for the trees." He snickered and eyed the surrounding trees.

I smiled. My problem might be the opposite. I didn't see the trees because I'd been hurt in the forest before. "You're right. I'm not ready for anything. He might be interested, but I don't know him."

Dad's expression sobered. "If you ever feel unsafe after he comes to camp, you tell me. I can hogtie him to a tree and we'll drive off."

The image his words gave me made me laugh. It'd been barely over twenty-four hours since he had collapsed, but it felt like humor had been absent from my life for years. "I don't know. He looks like he could bust out of his ropes."

Dad chuckled. "I'll use fishing line. That stuff only breaks when there's a fish on the end."

I barked out more laughter. Coming to visit him was more like a way to run away from my problems rather than to deal with them. But this moment confirmed I made the right decision.

Camping with Deacon for the next two days would be the conclusive answer about whether or not I made the worst mistake of my life.

CHAPTER
FIVE

va

WHEN DEACON SHOWED UP, I wasn't ready to be hit with his sheer masculine beauty.

Oh, I had seen how hot he was when I was panicking about my dad, but it didn't register. In the hospital, I was more in mental survival mode. He felt good to sleep on. He was nice to look at. I knew he was the best-looking guy I'd ever seen.

But Dad was safe. I was a single woman. And Deacon was *fine*. Under the sun, the caramel highlights in his hair shone against the darker mahogany strands. My fingers twitched with the urge to shove my hands into those locks and see how soft a man's hair could be.

The width of his shoulders could block out the sun when he stood in front of me, and the way he grinned, with that square jaw, could make Superman look like he was an amateur model.

Was I resisting an oath I swore to this guy?

I straightened my shoulders. No. I wasn't sacrificing my plans and my life for a guy who was probably fucking with me.

Deacon and Dad discussed where to set up Deacon's tent. Oath or not, I wasn't naively letting a man boss me around again. I wouldn't be treated like I was nothing and discarded like yesterday's trash. Chance found no value in our relationship and it was devastating. This god of a man would consume me, spit me out, and find himself a different treasure.

I was someone's treasure, and I was going to hold out until I was treated like it.

Dad waited to go fishing until Deacon arrived. He was more excited than I expected. Chance had never come home with me, so Dad already liked Deacon better than him. I went to the coolers lined up beside my tent to pack some snacks for us while we shore fished.

My hair got in the way when I bent over the coolers. I straightened and slipped a hair tie off my wrist. I gathered my hair in a ponytail and glanced at the guys. Deacon watched me, his eyes dark and filled with a promising heat.

My belly flipped, and I looked away. Why was he watching me? I used to try to dress nice. I had a collection of sexy lingerie, but I could've done a gymnastics routine in my lacy negligee and Chance wouldn't have been less impressed.

I had changed into one of Dad's old gray flannel shirts and a pair of old cutoff jeans. My hiking boots completed the lumbersexual style, and my hair was in a messy topknot. But Deacon looked at me like I was a mint chip ice cream cone and he wanted to lick me from head to toe.

How badly did I want to stick with my pride?

No, it wasn't a negotiation.

I loaded up two portable coolers, but I left Dad's six-pack in the big cooler. We weren't flirting with any more disaster today.

Dad gestured to Deacon. "He brought his own rod and bait."

A prepared fisherman. Maybe my dad could uphold the oath for me. "Sounds like we're ready then."

Deacon's low rumble wasn't aimed at me, but I felt it just the same when he said, "After you."

Dad took off down the gravel path that looped through the campsite. It'd take us to the main trail that led to the best places for shore fishing. Deacon was still watching me.

"You go ahead," I said. "You and Dad seem to have a lot of fishing to talk about."

"Your dad knows I'm not here to fish."

Shivers traced over my skin. I altered between sweltering hot and so cold that I wanted to move closer to him and capture his heat. With a huff, I started after Dad.

The stroke of Deacon's gaze on my ass was like a brand. It had to be my imagination. I had a plain ass. More of my Goldilocks syndrome—not too big, not too flat.

I couldn't explain why I put a little extra sway in my hips, but I did. A low rumble sounded behind me. I slowed until he was walking next to me. "Do you have a growling problem?"

"My kind makes sounds that might seem odd to humans."

"Like what?" Why did I continue to ask when I would not believe what he said?

"We try not to roar. It's not forbidden but we're very judicious with them. They can give us away."

Again, I was prompted to ask, "When would you need to roar?"

"To warn our people of danger. To signal a fight. A plea for help. Situations that aren't common today, but you never know."

He said it so easily. He believed what he was telling me, firmly planted in the fantasy world he built for himself.

The image of him kneeling over Dad floated to the surface of my mind. Doubt crept in. Deacon basically brought my dad back from the dead with nothing but a touch. That lent a lot of reality to the fantasy.

I'd reserve judgment until I saw more. "If humans don't know about you, who would you fight with?"

"Each other."

The shivers returned. "Why do you fight each other?"

He glanced at Dad who'd turned off the gravel path and was already on the trail. Dad didn't like to waste time when it came to getting hooks in the water. "We refer to the Jade clan as envies. They're jealous of the life we have. They're jealous of our fortune. They're jealous of our mates." He snapped his mouth shut and glared at the ground while he walked.

There was something about the mate thing he wasn't telling me. "What about the mates?"

"We'll have to talk about the envies soon, but not now."

I rolled my eyes as my temper got the best of me. I spoke quietly enough to keep Dad from hearing me. "If this is supposedly my life now, why do I have to ask so many questions? Why can't you tell me what I need to know? What's with being all cryptic and shit?"

The corner of his lip curled up. "I like your fire."

I made my own growling sound. "You didn't answer a damn thing."

"In due time, my golden-haired temptress. In due time."

I risked losing my balance on the uneven trail to gawk at him. "Never in my life has the word temptress been used in the same sentence as me."

"Then you've been hanging around the wrong kind." He feathered his fingers over a loose lock of hair from my topknot. "You are very tempting indeed."

Dad chose that moment to turn back, pointing to his right. "We'll head down there a ways. No one should bother us that far off the path."

"Looks like a great spot, Dorian," Deacon called.

I said nothing, just followed them. The talk about dragons and envies shattered his claims about how tempting I was. A little bit of hope, then he said wild shit.

DEACON

MY HUMAN WAS FLUSTERED. I sensed she was warming up to me. She tried to keep her dad between us, and she probably thought I didn't notice the furtive glances out of the corner of her eye, but I sensed the growing chasm was back.

My world was difficult for humans to believe, and

when we lived so much like them nowadays, revealing ourselves was harder than ever.

"You said something about a good walleye spot?" Dorian had found a spot big enough to fit the three of us side by side with a decent rock to sit on. He stuck the end of his rod between two rocks and let his line stay out for a while.

"I can take you both this afternoon or tomorrow."

The lake was close to my home. Fishing there would mean drawing Ava closer to my home. As much as I wanted to toss her over my shoulder and haul her away like the old days, I couldn't. I wouldn't. I wanted a mate who loved me, trusted me, not one who feared me.

She had no idea what defiance meant, how seriously my kind took oaths. I was trying to keep her from finding out, and we had a little time. Barely, but I'd use what I could.

"We'll see how today goes," Dorian answered, and I suspected he was talking about more than the fishing.

"Sounds good." I readied my line and studied the man who was so important to my mate.

Did she realize how much her dad relied on fishing? He enjoyed it, yes. She probably thought he was a fanatic. But I sensed the underlying reason for the despair inside of him. He was lonely. He was scared. Ava hadn't said what happened to her mother, but I sensed the same in many shifters who had lost mates.

The water calmed him. Fishing was an unchanging routine in a life that had irrevocably changed him. When he lay unconscious in the hospital room, I felt nothing from him but his heartbeat and his energy. When he woke up, that had changed to confusion and amazement as he heard the story of what had happened. On the outside, he was a pleasant man, mellow yet enthusiastic, who supported his daughter. And all that hid the pain.

The sharp sting of loss emanated from him. I would bet the only time he could sort out his thoughts was when he was by the water.

It was ironic I understood more than his own daughter would. Water was calming to our kind. Most of our clans were situated around a body of water. The special walleye place I told them about was practically my backyard. Silver Lake was on my family's land and even more peaceful than this one.

Excitement grew inside me. I'd always hoped my mate would find the area as special as I did.

I had tried with Venus. I showed her my home. The lake. My thinking spot. She'd been mildly interested, but no matter how long we'd known each other, she held herself at a distance. I didn't dislike her, but I wasn't drawn to her like Ava.

The attempt at making me and Venus a thing had been a failure from the beginning. Did she feel that way?

"Where is this place?" Ava asked suddenly, as if she'd been sitting on the question and tried to ignore her curiosity.

The corner of my mouth tipped up. She couldn't resist knowing more about life, even if it was through a lake she'd probably never heard about.

"It's about twenty minutes from Wildrose, right along the border." Technically, much of my family's land knew no border, but in order to stay under the radar, we respected human laws. "We can even camp there."

Excitement lit Dorian's face while Ava's mouth fell open. I wanted to claim those pretty pink lips and get my first sweet taste of her, but I jerked my attention away before I shamed myself in front of her father.

"There's camping?" she squeaked.

"It's pretty much my own backyard." I met her gaze and let a hint of my smugness shine through.

Dorian glanced at his daughter, oblivious to her distress. Or perhaps his fatherly instinct told him I was right for his daughter. "I don't think it'll hurt to move camp for the night."

"I don't want you to tax yourself after your collapse." The tang of Ava's genuine concern reached my nose. Dammit. She didn't know her father's heart was strong enough to tear down and set up camp every night for the next year. She didn't trust me enough for that yet. She was worried about him and about camping so close to me.

"I can help," I offered. "I only mean to show off the gems of the county." That might be a lie. I loved my home. But my goal was Ava.

Ava clenched her jaw and glowered at the water. "It's up to Dad. This is his vacation, but I'm going to make sure he doesn't exhaust himself again."

Her care for her father was very real. They were close, like I had been with my parents. A trait that was important to me. I'd lost my parents years ago—about the same time Venus lost hers. It'd been a fire, and many shifters—both Jade and Silver—suspected her brother.

I had my doubts. A guy who'd kill his parents in order to ascend to power would be a worse leader than they were. Yet Lachlan ruled his kind with an iron fist, but he never unfairly lashed out.

How would he react when I rejected his sister?

I didn't want conflict, but I couldn't give up on Ava.

Not because of the oath, but because she was mine. I'd given up a lot to lead my kind; I should be allowed to try to win over the one I wanted to spend my life with.

"Tearing down camp shouldn't be too hard," Dorian said, his gaze on the middle of the lake where he'd collapsed. This place was unnerving him. He sensed he'd been on death's door and he worried about his daughter. He was willing to accept the offer to go somewhere else from the stranger who'd saved him.

Ava would still fret over him. "All you need to do is pack your clothing. I'll take down the tents and load those up with the coolers. The only thing I want you to do is relax by the crystal-blue water and catch some walleye."

Ava shook her head, but Dorian slapped his knees. "Well, I can't pass up an amazing camping spot and an amazing fishing spot. Life's too short."

Ava's consternation morphed to understanding. Being back at the lake that had changed her life unsettled her, and her father's urgency to find somewhere else to be told her the same about him.

"You'll both enjoy it." The words *I promise* nearly slipped out. I'd do my best, but my main goal would be winning Ava over. I couldn't risk making another promise when the magnitude of Ava's oath hung over our heads.

CHAPTER

SIX

I was driving the pickup again and following Deacon in his. He had offered to have me ride with him. I continued to keep wanting to be flattered, but I couldn't let my guard down.

I thought Dad would ask to ride with Deacon, but he didn't. Dad got along with everyone, but he seemed fonder than usual of Deacon.

This lake better be spectacular.

Dad noticed my growing agitation. "You're sure you're okay with this?"

Guilt seeped in. Since Mom died, fishing saved Dad from long, dark winters. Ice fishing was too hard on him. He was limited to his favorite hobby for half the year before he had to sit inside and think about how he wouldn't be able to retire and travel in an RV.

Mom hadn't disliked camping or fishing, but she wasn't avid like Dad. She had enjoyed her time gardening and making crafts. Dad enjoyed the great outdoors. The winter had been their time together. They traveled south to warmer weather, or cuddled inside with cocoa and played board games. They had social groups for card games, walking socials in the mall each morning, and lunch dates with other retirees.

Winters were hard for Dad. I didn't want to go to Silver Lake, but I'd seen the same distraught expression on him when he looked at the lake. A change of location might be what he needed to keep the hobby that made his life worth living from getting ruined by a near-death experience.

"I'm only worried about you. The lake and everything sound nice." The way Deacon's handsome profile brightened while he described it softened the heart I was trying to protect from him.

"I haven't heard of Silver Lake. Must be a tiny little thing. But if the fishing is good and it's private, that'll be a treat."

I nodded as I slowed down. Deacon turned on to a county highway with no shoulder. We drove a few more miles surrounded by trees. Slowly, the fields for farming and ranching grew smaller until they ceased altogether. This area was almost too thick, too lush, for woods.

I'd only been over the border twice with my parents. We went to Winnipeg once, and then I did the obligatory *I'm eighteen and can legally drink in Canada trip with friends.* I didn't remember this many trees from the drive. It was like we were in another part of the country.

Deacon turned again, this time onto a gravel road that cut through the trees. It curved around and there was a glint of the blue between the leaves. I couldn't stare, otherwise I'd go off the road.

At least he hadn't lied about a lake.

Awe poured from Dad's voice. "That's not a small lake."

I grew up by Devils Lake, the largest natural lake in the state. I'd been with Dad to Lake Sakakawea, the largest man-made lake in the state. Silver Lake didn't compare to those, but it was no small watering hole.

I snuck glances while keeping my eye on the road. "How can this place not be inundated with people? It's too close to other recreation areas."

"He said it was on family property. Maybe that has something to do with it?"

"Maybe," I murmured. Or this lake could be just another detail about Deacon that made little sense.

The road looped around what I would assume was a portion of the lake. To our right, sparkling blue water could still be seen between the green leaves of the trees. But the vision to my left made me want to slam on my brakes.

"Holy Moses," Dad said as he twisted completely to the side. "Is that his house?"

Deacon pulled onto a narrow road that was more like a driveway. To my dismay, it was a driveway—that led right to the massive cabin.

"Maybe it's a lodge?" Wouldn't there be people wandering the grounds if this was a vacation spot? Where were the vehicles of the other guests? Would a lodge have a three-stall garage?

Deacon parked in a spot behind one of the garage stalls, and I parked next to him.

He killed the engine and hopped out. I kept Dad's

pickup running and rolled down the window. "Where are we?"

He raised his arms to encompass the property. Pride radiated like the afternoon sun from his grin. "My place."

"This is a home? Your home?" What did he do for a living? He said he was in charge of his people, and that he was a dragon. Did that come with a hoard?

"Welcome to my humble abode."

I refrained from rolling my eyes. Deacon hadn't been arrogant since I'd met him. He'd been confident and authoritative. But he wasn't exactly humble.

Deacon grabbed the coolers from the back of his pickup bed. By the time I got out of Dad's pickup, he hauled one in each hand. Dad didn't pack lightly, and Deacon's cooler was filled with enough meat to feed an army. Yet he acted as if they only weighed a few pounds.

"Since you're worried about your dad's exertion, I thought we could eat here. I've got a firepit in the back and a place we can clean the fish we caught this morning." He tilted his head in the direction of the lake. "There's no good parking around the shore, but it's not a far walk and the path isn't terribly technical. You'll still get a delightful afternoon of fishing if you want to go out again."

Dad grinned like Deacon just told him the winning lottery ticket was in his pocket.

My temper skyrocketed. I didn't like being manipulated. But my anger stalled. I was worried about Dad. Before the heart attack, there was a constant mantle of fatigue he wore around his shoulders. That was gone, but I couldn't shake the worry that it might come crashing back. A miracle happened thanks to Deacon, but I'd still have to watch my dad grow old without the love of his life.

Today wasn't that day. Dad was on an adventure and it was because of Deacon. This camping trip was as much about Dad as it was about me, and I had to act like it.

Dad circled to the back of the pickup. He reached into the box to grab the tents, but Deacon stopped him. "This place has more than enough bedrooms. You two are welcome to sleep in a real bed. Unless you want the Silver Lake camping experience, we can throw those up in the back."

Dad waved his hands in the air and practically danced to the front door. "I enjoy camping, don't get me wrong. But I've never stayed in a place like this."

Deacon hadn't moved. He still held the coolers like they were three-pound dumbbells.

"Was this part of your plan?" I asked, lacking the vitriol I had earlier.

"I'm trying to make this as painless for you as possible. You'll be more comfortable staying with me if you've been here with your dad and had a chance to experience the place as a guest."

"That's all I'll ever be," I warned.

Deacon's dark brows drew together. He lowered his voice. "Don't you realize, Ava, that all this is yours?"

I snorted, and Dad glanced back. He was already across the yard, ducking and bending to look at the logs of the cabin and the rock accents on the walls. I flashed him a quick smile. He went back to inspecting the flat, stacked rocks that made up the columns of the overhang. The massive porch had two rocking chairs angled toward each other. It must be nice to relax on those while watching the sunset.

I shook the thought out of my head. "None of this is mine. Do you expect me to believe that suddenly I'm half owner?"

"That's how it works with our kind."

"Good luck proving that the males of your kind are any different from mine." If a relationship made things half mine, I'd have a place to live. Chance wouldn't have been able to kick me out with nothing.

"I'm not some human male afraid of commitment."

"It's easy to commit when you're not giving up anything. What happens when you decide you're done with me? Are you going to boot me out and poof—I have nothing?"

The chiseled angles of his face hardened. "Don't make the mistake of comparing me to your ex."

"From where I'm standing, you're not much different from him." I could call it The Curse of Ava Payne: The girl who so desperately wanted the type of relationship her parents had had would only be teased with the possibility if she gave everything up. A memoir.

He set the coolers down and stalked toward me. I was trapped between the two vehicles. If I backed up, I'd hit the garage door.

Yellow flecks burned behind his blue irises. A wave of heat blasted off him. "If you knew the risks I'm taking to make you mine, you'd realize that there's nothing I'm not willing to do for you."

"You don't even know me." My heart rate kicked up. His intensity called to me on a visceral level. As a little girl, I dreamed of growing into a strong, independent woman. I also dreamed of having a man who wasn't intimidated by my side. Both dreams seemed like nothing more than a fantasy. I hated Deacon more for giving that little girl inside of me false hope.

The energy undulating around me vanished like he was the vacuum. The rigidness of his body drained away, and his eyes returned to their midsummer blue. Had I imagined it? "I want you and your dad to have a good time. It's important to me you like Silver Lake. You were worried about him, and I thought you'd appreciate that we wouldn't be setting up tents and tearing them down again. This way, he's not straining himself, and you and I can get to know each other."

These were the moments that made it so hard to tell him to fuck off. When he went from overbearing to sweetly considerate, I had a hard time walking away.

"Thank you for thinking of him," I said.

"As your mate, it's my job to take care of those who are important to you."

And there it was again. I was softening, and he ruined it by bringing up the whole mate thing.

I opened the back of the pickup to grab my duffel bag. "Just show me where I can put this stuff please." And then I'd shut my door and block out this man I couldn't seem to get away from.

DEACON

I WAS in the backyard with Dorian, cleaning and gutting fish. Ava was in the house getting settled. I wanted to watch her roam through my place. What were her reactions? Did she like the style? Was it too plain, too masculine, or did she have ideas of what she'd do with it? But ultimately, I wanted her to feel like it was hers, or that it could be hers, and I thought that would be easier if she didn't have me spying on her.

Dorian moved his hand like he was going to adjust the bill of his cap, but realized fish guts were all over his skin. I gestured to a sink in the corner of the little cleaning area. My entire back patio area was an outdoor kitchen with seating. I had a big house, but like most shifters, I liked big open spaces. The less my kind had been able to fly, the more we sought the freedom of the great outdoors.

Dorian rinsed his hands off. "I would've thought Ava would be out by now. But she was never into the cleaning side of fishing." He chuckled as he shook his hands dry. "She's not really into the fishing side of fishing either."

Ava would fish for weeks in order to hang out with her father, that much was clear. He meant a lot to her. "It's all right. I've been too forward with her and I think she needs her space." As soon as I showed her the guest bedroom she could sleep in, that was conveniently across the hall from mine, she shut the door and I hadn't seen her since.

"You seem like a nice guy, but she's my daughter. I only want the best for her."

I heard everything he didn't say. If the best for Ava was to be left alone, then he'd pack her up and go. If Ava didn't want me hitting on her, he'd help her load her things in the middle of the night when they thought I was sleeping and drive away. He wanted the best for his daughter, but he didn't realize that fulfilling her oath would be the best. It would be the safest.

I was the leader of Silver clan, and my people would

rectify a broken oath to honor their leader. I didn't want to think about what the other clans would do if they learned that not only did I break a contract with Jade clan, but I let a human ignore her oath to me.

"I knew there was something special about her the first time I saw her." I wasn't lying. Since her scream echoed across the lake, my inner beast had been riveted on her.

Dragons didn't have fated mates. It would make things easier. We were drawn to certain people, but there was no one mate. Venus was gorgeous, and I was considered attractive. I'd known her my entire life, but that didn't mean that I had an innate urge to spend the rest of my life living with her.

Ava's quiet beauty, the fire inside of her, and the way she cared for her dad were all signs that she was someone I could spend centuries with and not get bored.

"Well" —he adjusted the brim of his ball cap— "that ex of hers did a number on her, and it's barely been a week since they broke up."

Surprise ricocheted through my veins. "A week?"

The ex's scent would still be on her if they were that serious, and she'd only been apart from him for mere days. She was my cherry almond dessert that didn't stink of another man.

Dorian nodded as he studied the pile of white fish meat we built up. "She lost her job—downsizing—the day after he broke up with her and kicked her out of their apartment. Hit my poor girl pretty hard." Sadness traced through his features. "She'd probably have held up better if she had her mother to talk to, but we lost Dana over two years ago. Ava hasn't said anything, but she's a lot like me, and it feels like yesterday."

I felt the same about my parents.

"I've never really been in a relationship." This was the type of conversation I couldn't have with my father, as much as I had loved him. He believed in obligation and fulfilling one's purpose. He had been hopelessly in love with my mother, and he'd wanted to replicate that for me with Venus. Peace between our clans and true love? What could go wrong?

Absolutely zero chemistry between me and Venus.

"You don't seem like a lone wolf." Dorian wiped off his fillet knife.

"I don't want to be a lone wolf."

He didn't know how much like a lone wolf I would be if I wasn't mated by my birthday. I watched lone wolves closely and ordered a hit on them if it was necessary. Shifters without a pack were a dangerous thing, and it didn't matter the species. Shifters without a mate were nearly as dangerous.

"I've never found anyone who is okay just being with me. My job can be demanding, and I can't help but bring it home. I have siblings I can talk to. I'm a mayor, but I'm also the guy everyone goes to in Silver Lake when there's an issue. We're too small to have full-time law enforcement." That part was intentional, but he didn't have to know the intricacies. "It's kind of a family business. I don't want my mate—my partner—to get absorbed into my work. I want to come home and just be." I want to be plain old Deacon Silver with my mate.

"That makes sense. I don't understand what you do, but I've known guys like you. Keeping a professional life and a private life separate is important to them."

Those couldn't be separated for me, not in the way Dorian was assuming, but he was close enough. I had my brothers, Silver clan's council, and the entire clan with their nose in my business, questioning my decisions.

"I like you, Deacon. You're nothing like Ava's ex." He shook his head, his mouth turned down in a frown. "I tried hard to like that boy, to see what my daughter saw in him, but I couldn't escape the arrogance coming off him. I never gave much thought to narcissists, but I reckon he's it. You don't give off those vibes." He put his tools down. "But I will support my daughter and if she wants nothing to do with you, we'll leave, and I'd be mighty disappointed if you fought us."

It was a subtle warning, but it was there. Dorian didn't know that he didn't stand a chance against me. I was younger, I was stronger, and I grew up learning how to fight. He might sense all that, but he was still willing to place himself between me and Ava.

"I'm going to do everything I can to win over your daughter."

That was as much as I could say without lying. As the leader of my clan, I made a pact with them and myself that I would never lie. I forced Ava into an oath she had zero information about before she made it. She became mine when she uttered the words. Her life and well-being had become my responsibility as soon as I forced her to do it.

~

AVA

I DIDN'T KNOW what else to do while Deacon and Dad were outside cleaning fish. Deacon had mentioned grilling, but there was nothing Dad loved more than a beer-battered and deep-fried slab of walleye. Deacon deferred to me for the process.

The conversation reminded me of when I told Chance about how Dad's favorite food was fish he caught. My ex had made some condescending comment about Dad's country taste.

The longer I was away from the city, and the more I was around Deacon, had shown me how blatantly disrespectful Chance was. And I had stayed with him for years.

But Chance was nice in the beginning, just like Deacon. I couldn't let self-recrimination affect my judgment.

I stirred up the batter for the fish. Deacon's kitchen was modern with an intuitive layout. I could spend hours in here. I loved to cook and bake, but I hadn't done much since I left home. I was too busy in college, and then too afraid to make something that didn't meet Chance's standards.

Fuck Chance and his opinions. I let him dictate what I did and how I did it for too long.

Everything was ready for cooking as soon as the guys came through the sliding door. I turned from the stove and smiled at Dad, but my gaze was drawn to Deacon and the appreciative way he looked at me. The smug glint was back in his eyes. I was in his kitchen, about to cook for him.

The cavewoman in me elbowed the progressive girl out of the way.

He held up a plateful of white fillets. "I have the meats."

I couldn't stop myself from giggling. A man that

handsome and demanding shouldn't have a sense of humor too.

"The oil should be hot in just a few minutes. I can get these battered."

Deacon set the plate down, and Dad washed his hands. Deacon did the same. As he was drying his hands off, he asked, "What can I help with?"

God, he helped in the kitchen too? I was having a harder time finding a reason to back out on my supposed oath. Maybe I could stick around to see how things went. I could always leave when I knew for sure it wouldn't work.

No, I was not being forced to change my plans again. I was spending the rest of the week and most of the next with Dad, and then I was going home to look for a job. I'd call Avril and ask her if I could stay with her while I look for a new job.

Avril's boyfriend was kind of a dick, but he shouldn't have issues with me staying for a couple of weeks until I found a place.

I shoved my housing concerns out of the way. I wouldn't miss the chance to put Deacon to work. "You can start on whatever we're going to have with the fish."

"I'm a meat and more meat kind of guy, but I think I have some frozen hash browns I can fry up."

The joke was on me. There was only one stove. So that meant Deacon would park his big body right next to me while I cooked the fish and he made the hash browns. "How about a vegetable?"

He gave me a sexy smirk that made my knees go rubbery. If I didn't concentrate on what I was doing, I was going to hurt myself on the hot oil.

He crossed to the fridge and opened it. "Dorian, I have

some sad, wilted vegetables in here. Do you think we can do anything with them?"

Dad beamed and peered into the fridge. Deacon knew all the right things to say to my father. I both loved and hated him for it.

"Oh," Dad said, his tone excited about the challenge. "This is like the early days when Dana and I got married. We could only afford the discounted produce, but we learned some tricks over the years." He practically shouldered Deacon out of the way.

Deacon didn't bother to hide his smile since Dad's back was to him as he riffled through the fridge.

I could ignore what he did, or I could acknowledge my appreciation. "Thank you," I mouthed.

He lifted his chin like it was no big deal. I hadn't seen Dad so happy since before Mom got sick. Not even when he and I first began this camping trip. Dad's health and his improved mood were from Deacon.

I couldn't ignore that. If I was going to make a serious decision, then I needed to factor in Deacon's entire personality. I'd have to legitimately get to know him.

Why did my mood improve once I decided to give him a chance?

SEVEN

I couldn't say the exact moment a change came over Ava, but it was while we were all working together in the kitchen. Normally, I made a roast, grilled some meat, Crock-Pot*ted* meat, braised meat, seared, anything that could be done to meat, I did. I didn't spend a lot of time on the extras unless I was particularly hungry. Dragons were hearty carnivores. We burned off carbs too quickly. Fats were also a heavy part of our diet, and it was a lot easier to blend in since the rise of the Paleo diet, Atkins diet, Keto—if it was carb-free, we acted like we followed it.

I had never enjoyed making a meal before. Food was sustenance. Tonight, food was pleasure. But not as much as preparing a meal with people I enjoyed being around, then eating it around the table with them instead of listening to a message left by the council about the next feral shifter I'd have to deal with.

I was helping Ava with the dishes. She insisted on washing what couldn't be put in the dishwasher, and I dried and put them away. Dorian loaded the dishwasher with the plates and silverware and glasses and started it.

"The day kind of got away from us." I hooked the dish towel over a drawer knob. "We didn't get to Silver Lake. Do you want to go tonight?"

I had work to do. Emails needed answering. The number of messages I had on my phone climbed higher every hour, and I had some contracts to comb through. I'd been gone from work for a couple of days. Unheard of for me. With my thirty-fifth birthday bearing down on me, it was important for me to woo Ava.

Dorian ran a hand through his graying hair. "I'd love to, but I don't want to feel rushed. As much as I love fishing, I can only take cleaning fish once per day."

I chuckled but kept my attention on Ava without staring at her. If we didn't go to Silver Lake, that meant we were staying here. We'd had an enjoyable meal, and I learned more about Dorian's life as an insurance agent, but I wanted to get to know her. Staying in would be perfect for that, unless she shut herself in the guest bedroom. I wouldn't win her over by busting down the door and claiming that I just wanted to talk.

"I might just hit the hay," Dorian said. "Ava got me one of those e-readers, and I downloaded a few mystery novels before the trip."

"Not a problem." I didn't give Ava a chance to say she was doing the same thing. "Want to find a movie to watch? I get excellent service this far out of town."

A fleeting moment of panic went through her expression. Then resolve filled her eyes. "Sure, yeah. A movie sounds nice."

Triumph pumped through my veins, and I fought a wide grin.

"I'll leave you two to it," Dorian said as he shuffled out of the room. "The trip to Silver Lake sounds perfect for the morning."

"We'll be ready." It felt natural to talk like Ava and I were a unit. Ava didn't bristle, but perhaps she didn't realize what I had done.

She wiped her hands off on the towel. "What kind of movies do you like?"

I leaned my butt against the counter. She was staring out the window over the sink. I knew every square inch of what she was seeing. Tall trees, freshly mowed green grass, my firepit, the cleaning station. She could pick any window in this house and the view would be gorgeous. I wanted her to like it as much as I did.

"I'll watch whatever you want."

She rolled her eyes toward me. "Are you always going to let me get my way if I stay here with you?"

"Yes," I answered simply.

She watched me for several seconds as if she was waiting for me to laugh it off as a joke. I wasn't joking. Ava would be saving my life, but that wasn't why I had the urge to do whatever she asked. There was a drive inside of me I couldn't quiet. I wanted to please her, and I wanted to pleasure her, and I was desperately trying to keep my mind off the latter. The direction my thoughts were taking would definitely scare her off.

She gave her head a little shake. "Let's just pick a movie."

I led her to my den downstairs, ducking into my office

for my computer as we went. She chose the overstuffed chair to sit in, a single-seater. I took the end of the couch closest to her.

I scrolled through all of our options.

"I can't believe you have all this," she said.

"I've never had a problem with reception out here. Dragons' love for gems is helpful when it comes to paying for top quality services."

Her brow furrowed when I mentioned dragons, but she ignored it. "Whoa, I haven't seen the new Marvel movie."

"You like action hero movies?" There was probably no correlation, but if she could watch a teenage kid with spider abilities swinging through New York, then the idea of shifters shouldn't seem too far fetched.

"Doesn't everybody?"

"I don't know. I've never watched one."

Her eyes widened, and she stared at me like I was from another planet. I'd told her I could shift into a dragon, but she was more disbelieving that I hadn't seen a Marvel movie yet.

"Oh, then we need to go back to the first one."

"No. I'm catching up on work, so you watch what you want. We can watch the first movie another time."

Her gaze shifted to me, but she didn't react otherwise. "All right." She curled her legs underneath herself.

I tossed her a throw blanket that my mother had gotten for me when I first built this cabin. Ava spread it over her lap and burrowed deeper into the cushions. Watching her in my kitchen had satisfied my dominant urge to fully claim her. But it was nothing like seeing her make herself at home.

"Why are you looking at me like that?"

I answered honestly. "I like seeing you in my house, using my things—we like to please our mates, and that includes basic comfort."

"I'll bite," she muttered. "So this mate thing, how does it work between shifters and humans? Like, do dragon shifters or whatever take human mates? Are you immortal or something?"

"My kind agreed to give up our immortality in order to accept humans as our mates."

Disbelief touched her gaze. "So at some point, you were immortal?"

"That was eons ago. I come from a long line of mortals."

"Was the exchange worth it?"

She was asking questions. That had to be a good sign. "Our numbers were dwindling. Immortality can make one lazy. It's counterintuitive, but after living on your own terms for a few centuries, I heard it was hard to adjust to mates."

She considered it. "That made sense. Some of my old coworkers are almost forty, and they desperately wanted to meet the person of their dreams, but every time they dated someone promising, the relationship dissolved. My coworkers weren't willing to compromise parts of their lives they thought were critical to their happiness, but at the same time they refused to change their ways, and that included putting the toilet seat down or cleaning the hair out of the drain."

"I will clean the drains; you don't need to do that. Unless you want to."

She blanched. "I'm all about equal opportunity, but I vomit with too-clogged drains."

My laughter earned a smile from her. "Don't worry,

I've seen some disgusting things in my life. A clogged drain is no problem."

She lifted her chin toward my laptop. "Do you work from home?"

"Technically, no." I opened the computer and turned it on. I didn't care at the moment if I got one single task completed. "Silver Lake has a city hall. On paper, I'm the mayor and there's a city council. We rule Silver clan, and therefore we rule all the clans."

"That's the hierarchy?"

I nodded. "Silver is at the top, followed by the gemstone clans."

"You're the only metal?"

"It sets us apart that way. We don't have a clan for every gemstone. I honestly don't know the rhyme or reason behind our titles, but I would guess it's based mostly on our coloring." I waved a hand around my body. "My family, and other members born into the clan, have a silver gleam to our scales. The Jade clan is green, the Ruby clan reddish, and so on. And we're dragons, so gems make sense."

"You're dragons and you have a hoard," she said with a giggle.

I stared at her. Was she cracking up over an old stereotype that turned out to be true? My lips twitched. Her laughter grew.

"You have, like, a pile of diamonds under your cushion? Or emeralds hidden under the kitchen sink?"

"When we talk about our wealth, we're not usually met with laughter. But yes, I do have my fair share of gems. Over the years, most of it has been converted to money so we can invest. Even dragons know that our wealth can grow better in the stock market than under our mattress."

Her laughter faded, but her smile remained. I liked her smile. Her eyes lit up, and the stress and insecurity lining her face disappeared. She was as radiant as any gem I had ever owned.

"Want me to show you?" I asked.

"Show me the emeralds hidden under your bathroom sink or your stock portfolio?"

I chuckled. "I can show you both. They're equally impressive."

She laughed again.

I rose and beckoned her to follow me. I ducked into my office, turning the light on. I went to the safe in the corner and entered the code.

When she saw what I was doing, she said, "Oh, no. You don't literally have to show me. That you have a ton of diamonds and gemstones stashed around your house is easier to believe than most of what I've heard since I met you."

I peered at her over my shoulder. "Are you turning me down right before I show you my prize package?"

Her cheeks blazed pink. A nervous giggle escaped her. "When you put it like that, show me your package."

I grinned as I dug out a little pouch. This was why I waited so long, risking my life and my standing in the clan. I wanted a partner who was easy—easy to be around, easy to make laugh, and easy to fall in love with. All I had to do now was convince her that her oath to me was the easiest decision she ever had to make.

∼

AVA

DEACON DUMPED a velvet pouch of mixed gems into his big palm. Facets of colored light decorated his skin.

"They're gorgeous," I breathed. I touched the tip of my finger to a square ruby. Snatching my hand back, I said, "I'm sorry. I should have asked first."

"That's the one that drew your interest first?" he said, like he didn't mind at all.

I suppressed a smile. I wasn't expecting lightness and laughter when I agreed to watch a movie with him. This night had taken a different turn than I expected. "Would I offend you if I said I was partial to rubies?"

He plucked the jewel out and held it up to the light between his thumb and forefinger. The stone was gorgeous. My parents had given me jewelry on special occasions. A Black Hills gold cross for my eighth birthday. A pearl necklace when I graduated. And Mom insisted I take her wedding band, but I kept it at Dad's place. She'd said there was no need to bury something special in the ground when someone could still get some joy out of it. I loved that wedding band. I hoped to wear it one day and be as happy as my parents were.

"Hold your hand out."

I did as he asked, excited that I might get to hold the ruby. He placed it in my palm.

"It's just gorgeous." I lifted my hand to peer closer. "Look at all that detail. This must be worth a fortune." I wouldn't tell him I thought his jewel collection was cool. It's not something I expected someone to have, and it was a fairly unique item to collect. Diamonds, sapphires, emeralds, and rubies. He probably had stones I had never heard of before.

He shook the rest of the stones back into the pouch and drew the string closed. "It's yours."

I nearly dropped the gem. I closed my fingers around it to keep from losing it. "What?"

"It's yours. I can get a pouch for you to put it in. You can start your own hoard or have it placed in a setting." He traced the rough pad of his fingertip over my collarbone. "I think it would look lovely in a ring."

I thrust my hand toward him. "No, I can't possibly accept this."

He gripped my wrist and stroked his thumb over my pulse point. I didn't know when we got so close, but I had to tilt my head to look up at him. The heat in his gaze zeroed in on me. "Do you have any idea how it makes a male feel to give his mate a precious gem? Do you have any idea how much pleasure I'm getting from watching you gush over my stones?"

"I... I don't... I've never owned something worth that much. Most of my car is still owned by the bank."

A low rumble emanated from his chest. "Then let me do this."

"We're not even together."

Irritation flashed through his gaze, but I thought I caught a hint of panic. He stroked a finger down my cheek. "While I'm grateful that you're not the type of girl that can be bought, I don't like hearing you say we're not together. I want you, Ava."

"Why?" I breathed. "I'm just some girl. You haven't seen me at my best, but you definitely haven't seen me in the morning after a shitty night's sleep when I'm cranky and haven't showered yet."

His low chuckle was soothing to my ears. I liked the nonverbal sounds this man made. What did that mean about me?

He leaned his head down until his lips were inches from my ear. "Now is probably not the time to tell you that shifters have sharper senses and that your smell delights me very much."

I choked on a simple breath of air. "You can smell me?" I was half joking about how he hadn't seen me at my worst, but I wasn't sure I wanted him to smell me at my okayest.

He dropped his head farther. "Oh, yes, Ava. I can smell you, but what I really want to do is taste you."

I made the mistake, or maybe it was intentional and I damn well knew it, of turning my head up just as he tilted his chin down. Our lips met, and he pulled me closer. The ruby was still clutched in my fist, and my hand was smashed between our bodies as he took more from the kiss. Or did I give it to him?

He was warm and masculine and this kiss was like nothing I'd experienced before. He commanded me. I opened my mouth for him when I sensed he wanted it opened. I answered the strokes of his tongue with mine. I made a sound that was something between a moan and a whimper, and I clutched his shoulder with my free hand.

His embrace tightened and he picked me up. A simple turn and my ass landed on the top of his desk. I automatically parted my legs to make room for his body.

God, that felt good. His big size between my thighs. The way he dominated something as simple as a kiss. And I couldn't ignore the heavy bulge pressed against my lower stomach.

He was doing something sinful with his tongue, like

he was mimicking the act of sex, and this could be enough to bring me to orgasm. Whatever he was doing, I was on board.

He tipped me back. Either my abs were going to give out or I could just as well give up and lie across his desk. I put my hands down to steady myself. The ruby I had forgotten about clinked against the top of the desk and rolled across the surface.

I ripped my mouth off his. "Oh, no. Oh." The gem had bumped against a notepad. We were making out in his office. The door was open and my dad slept down the hall. Where was my restraint? Flustered, I pushed him away and rushed for the door. "Thank you, but I can't accept it. Sorry."

I darted out of the room like the coward I was and didn't stop until I was behind the closed door of the guest room. My heart rate was through the roof and I stood with my back against the door, waiting to catch my breath.

I touched my fingers to my sensitive lips. How in the world was I going to sleep tonight?

CHAPTER
EIGHT

Deacon

THE NEXT MORNING, as soon as my eyes opened, I swung my legs off the side of the bed and sat there. After that kiss with Ava, I didn't have enough brainpower to comprehend what I was supposed to be doing today.

The panicked look in her eyes after she dropped the ruby was emblazoned into my brain. Her reaction to me had been strong and unexpected—for both of us. It was all I could do not to chase after her. But I talked that part of my beast down. My mate was distressed, but hunting her down wouldn't help.

Her ex had hurt her. If I could, I'd resurrect one of our old laws and challenge him to the death. But our kind no longer did that.

She might be resisting the oath based on principle,

but what we were doing on the desk was raw. It was real. There was a strong part of her holding herself back.

I was running out of time. I would have to make the most of today and tomorrow.

Sounds from the kitchen pricked my eardrums. A glass getting taken out of the cupboard. A bowl being set on the counter. The squeak of the egg carton as it was taken out of the fridge.

It was Dorian. When Ava worked in the kitchen, she had a flow. Her movements were like a melody, a tune that matched my own.

I couldn't tell if Ava was awake, and I couldn't put my ear to the door to listen to her breathing. Getting caught would be a definite setback.

I got up, dressed in jeans, a white T-shirt, and a loose flannel to go fishing.

In the hallway, I ran into Ava coming out of her room. She stopped abruptly, her gaze shifting to the wall. The heat of her blush only made her cherry almond scent stronger.

"Morning," I rumbled.

"Morning."

I could've let her go about her business, but I was content to soak in her presence. She'd pulled her hair back into a ponytail, but it was her clothing that might require me to duck back into my room.

As if it wasn't bad enough battling an erection after our kiss in my office, I had lost precious amounts of sleep trying to reroute blood to the rest of my body. I refused to jack off in the shower. The only way I wanted to relieve myself was in her body. I would be patient.

But the athletic leggings hugging her generous curves and the way her pink T-shirt curved over her breasts were all I could concentrate on. It was a good thing she was facing me. If I got a glimpse of her ass encased in those leggings, I might have to break my personal oath of not masturbating in the shower.

"Sorry, did you need the bathroom?" she asked.

"There's a master bath in my bedroom." With a soaking tub big enough for the both of us. I could imagine her on top of me like she had been in the hospital—

I lurched down the hallway. Hopefully, she wouldn't think I was rude, but if I stood next to her any longer and had more thoughts about her sharing a bath with me, I was going to humiliate myself in front of her and probably piss her dad off.

In the kitchen, Dorian was whisking eggs. My stomach rumbled. I should tell him to make the entire dozen. That was what I usually ate myself, but I could ration to look a little more normal around them. I went to the fridge and dug out two ropes of Polish sausage. A hungry dragon is an angry dragon, so I couldn't hold back that much.

"I didn't know how much you wanted me raiding your fridge," Dorian said with a sheepish smile.

"My home is your home, but I've got an enormous appetite."

He chuckled. "If I had all your muscles, I'd eat as much as I could too. I'm standing here doubting how many of these eggs I should have after my medical adventures."

I couldn't tell Dorian that his arteries were as clear as a cloudless sky in the middle of June or that his heart would last for four more decades if he wanted to see what the other side of a hundred years old looked like. But I kept my mouth shut. I'd have plenty of problems if Ava broke her oath. There was no need to look for more.

~

Ava

Fishing at Silver Lake was more fun than I expected. I thought I would be more suspicious of Deacon after our kiss last night, but I was more relaxed than I had been in weeks.

The lake had plenty of walleye, true to Deacon's word. I hadn't seen Dad this giddy since before Mom passed away.

Dad laughed, took his hat off and ran a hand through his gray hair, and stuffed it back in place. "I feel guilty. Three of us catching our limit before noon?"

My fishing skills were as dismal as ever. My contribution was to increase our limit via my presence. Technically, I didn't catch all of my limit, but that was the story we were going to tell if anyone official asked. Deacon didn't seem worried. If he was the mayor, then maybe he wasn't worried about game wardens, but I was.

Deacon finished securing his hook and put his rod down. "Should we cook up the fish for lunch or supper?"

I eyed the fish in our water bucket. "I think it might be both."

We cruised through a lot of fish last night, but a third of this pile was Deacon's. He was letting us stay at his place and fish in his secret spot. I didn't want to eat him out of the stash and we couldn't take any with us.

I didn't want to go.

A spear of anxiety tore through me. One kiss and I was ready to change all my plans. "You'll have a nice stash of fish to freeze after we leave."

Deacon's blue gaze sharpened on me. "Or you can stay and help me finish it."

My dad rescued me from having to answer. "Be careful what you promise an old man. I might just take you up on it and see if it's possible for a person to get sick of their favorite food."

Deacon's gaze didn't leave me as his full lips spread into an affable grin. "I think you might fish all the walleye out of the lake before you get sick of it."

"Don't forget the trout," I added, grateful for the easy atmosphere between us despite the whole mate thing.

I packed up our gear and loaded the rods in the fishing boxes in the back of Deacon's pickup. I left the fish for the guys.

My stomach was rumbling on the drive back to his cabin. I was sitting in the front with him, and like he had the advanced hearing he said he had, he glanced at me. "Sounds like we'll have to save the fish for tonight and feed you as soon as we get home."

"No, it's fine. I can wait. Maybe I can even look up a new recipe."

"You can do that while we clean the fish, but I'll throw something else in the oven." The same heat from last night infused his eyes. "Can't have my woman be hungry, now can I?"

My cheeks flamed, and I couldn't suppress a smile. If Dad heard him, he didn't say anything. But then Dad seemed to be on Team Deacon.

I planned to tell him I would look for something to throw in the oven when he turned down his drive. A cherry red sports car sat on the concrete pad in front of his garage.

The rumble that came from Deacon wasn't like the one I'd heard last night. This was more like a groan.

"Who's that?" I asked.

Deacon's hand tightened on the steering wheel, his stare aimed at the car. The driver's door opened and a statuesque blonde unfolded her long body from the driver's seat. Dirty-blonde hair with platinum highlights and dyed green tips was piled on top of her head. I couldn't make a messy topknot look that stylish if I paid two hundred dollars to have someone else do it. The shorts she wore barely covered her ass cheeks, leaving long golden legs.

It was a surprise how much I could envy another person. The woman was beautiful, but when she pushed her aviator shades to the top of her head and saw us driving in, she crossed her arms that had enough muscles to bench press me. Her expression turned to stone.

Shivers worked over my body. This woman was intimidating.

"That's Venus," Deacon said flatly.

"She's stunning."

"She knows it." His tone was grim, like he was driving us straight into battle. And from the look on her face, I expected war on the horizon.

"Are you two a thing?"

"No, but there's a story I have to tell you." His tone said I wouldn't like the story.

The woman continued to stare at us as Deacon parked next to her car. Deacon was the first to get out, holding his hands up like he was trying to calm her before she said a word.

Dad opened his door and slid out. "I'll take the fish into the back and start cleaning them."

I helped Dad get the supplies he needed out of the back of the pickup.

He put a hand on my shoulder. "If we need to leave, you just say so," he whispered.

The sun beat down on the top of my head and my shoulders, but ice lined my veins. This was who Deacon was supposed to be with? I couldn't imagine any guy turning her down, especially not for me.

This confrontation wasn't my concern, but I couldn't shake the sense of obligation I had to stay and explain to Venus that I was not fighting for any man.

"Go ahead, Dad. It'll be all right."

He disappeared around the side of the house, and I dragged my leaden feet to stand by Deacon and Venus.

"A human, really?" Venus hissed. Her eyes were a brilliant shade of emerald that matched the dye in her hair.

After seeing this woman next to Deacon, I couldn't lie and say it didn't look like they belonged together.

Venus's voice shook as she said, "You're sworn to me."

"You're engaged?" I sputtered. Of course he was taken. What was I thinking? He hadn't hopelessly fallen for me. He had her.

Deacon kept his voice low as he responded. "I made no such oath."

"I didn't either. Use that excuse and see how far it gets you."

My patience snapped. They were sworn to each other, but neither of them had agreed to it? Was I the only one who supposedly promised anything? "How are you two engaged, but neither of you agreed to it?"

Deacon's hard edges softened when he glanced at me.

"Our clan councils made the arrangement and our parents agreed."

"What is it with you people making promises for others? Glad to hear it's not just the women who get forced into promises." I made a disgusted noise. "It's messed up. You shouldn't be forced to marry people you don't want to."

"The little human knows nothing about our kind." She tilted her head and studied me like there was a microscope lens between us. "Yet you're standing up for me? Don't you want him?"

Oh, I wanted him. If I had caught one glimpse of him at any point in my life before Dad collapsed, I would've wanted him so badly my chest ached. But I'd know it was a fantasy. My emotions wouldn't be getting toyed with like they were now. "I want to do what's best for *me* in life and not what some guy thinks is best."

Venus studied me, mint green nails tapping her chin. "You're not going to get that here, little human. Deacon and his brothers will rule your life."

"Venus," Deacon growled.

Venus rolled her eyes to him. "Am I wrong? Just because you don't have the balls to tell her what living in our world is really like doesn't mean I'll stay quiet."

"By now, no one expects you to stay quiet."

The dynamics between these two weren't sizzling chemistry. If I didn't know better, I would think they were impossibly gorgeous siblings. No wonder each of them was chafing so hard at being ordered to marry.

"News of you camping out in the hospital with a human travels fast. You should've known my brother would be bombarded with gossip." Venus snatched her sunglasses off her head and folded them. "For once, it seems people were correct. When were you going to tell me you're trying to find another mate in the last ten yards?"

Deacon's shoulders sagged with a sigh. "I'm sorry, Venus. I should've told you. I know you don't want the contract between us either, but I've only known Ava a couple of days and she's new to everything. I wanted to be certain before I approached our councils."

Hearing him talk to another person about councils and marriage contracts was trippy. What were the odds more than one person believed a delusional fantasy?

"They're going to shit themselves. We were supposed to be the union that brought peace."

"Do you really think members of your clan will quit vandalizing Silver property?"

"Doesn't matter what I think." Her matter-of-fact tone made me look underneath her beauty. Her eyes shone with a low-level anxiety that I had a feeling was always present. The way she stood was as in your face as it was defensive. She reminded me of Avril. Defiant and rebellious out of necessity.

"Well, you're here now. Might as well stay and keep everyone guessing about what's going on. I want as much time with Ava as I can get. To make sure she's comfortable."

Suspicion darkened the green of her eyes. "What aren't you telling me?" She glanced between us. "I'll get it out of her."

Deacon edged between me and Venus, his body tense, like he was ready for a fight. "You're not going to touch her."

Venus rolled her eyes and met my gaze. "You don't seem exactly enthralled with Deacon. Otherwise, he wouldn't be hiding you." She patted his chest, but nothing about her touch was sexual. "He's a real Boy Scout. If he didn't run to his council to tell them about you, then he fucked up and he's trying to make it right."

I chewed on my lower lip. Venus was startlingly observant. I exchanged a look with Deacon, and he answered. "Her dad was in trouble. I saved him in exchange for her oath to be mine."

Venus made a choking sound. "You did what?" She stared at him, blinking several times.

A sense of validation sifted through my mind. What he had done wasn't ordinary. I was caught in a web of rules I knew nothing about.

"I'm trying to make it right." He slid an arm around my waist. "She called to me."

Venus arched a questioning brow at me.

I shrugged, like what do you do?

"Yeah, I'm going to take you up on your offer. I've gotta see how this plays out." She tossed her sunglasses into her car. As she slammed the door shut, she and Deacon jerked around to look down the driveway.

What now? I turned to see what was going on. The drive was empty, then a few seconds later, a pickup turned in.

Had they heard the engine? Was their hearing really that good? I was beginning to believe more and more of what they said.

"What are they doing here?" Irritation dripped from Venus's voice.

"My brothers are welcome here at all times." But his tone said this was a bad fucking time.

"What's the point of living on your own if you can't forbid family from stopping by?" Her question wasn't rhetorical. Deacon didn't answer. What were his brothers like?

The heels of her wedge sandals clicked against the concrete as she stormed into the house.

How often had she been here?

Jealousy sizzled in my belly. I took measured breaths to make it go away. I didn't like feeling like this. Nothing about the way they acted together gave me cause to be jealous—and I shouldn't care anyway.

He rested a big hand on the middle of my back. "What's wrong?"

"Nothing but the mess you got me into." I would never tell him how I really felt.

The guy driving the pickup was the brother from the day Dad collapsed. I remembered little more than the terror. Had I gotten his name?

"Steel," Deacon greeted. "What are you and Penn up to today?"

The second brother got out. He was as tall and strikingly handsome as Deacon and Steel, but something about him resonated as younger. I would guess he was closer to my age.

Penn's gaze strayed in the direction Venus had gone. "We saw a certain little red car drive through town. Steel told me what happened a few days ago, and we figured the two situations were going to clash." He lifted a brow as if to confirm whether the situations had clashed.

I was tempted to take offense at being referred to as a situation, but something about Penn's tone soothed any defense that had risen. He wasn't exactly concerned about me, but I didn't get the impression he was terribly worried about his brother.

Was he wondering how Venus handled it?

The blue in Penn's eyes swirled darker the longer he stared at the house. Did he have a thing for Venus?

Interesting.

"Everything's fine." Deacon's response lacked confidence. "You all might as well come in to eat. You can help Ava's dad clean fish."

CHAPTER
NINE

eacon

"You guys catch up. I'll go help Dad." Ava stormed in the same direction her father had gone in.

The Venus meet and greet could've been worse, but it could've been better. My brothers' arrival would not make this easier. "Venus was surprisingly chill about it. But she figured out that I forced Ava into the oath."

"Have you told Ava what it means?" Steel asked.

"I haven't discussed the specifics with her."

"That's pretty fucked up, Deacon," Penn said.

I shoved my fingers through my hair and snarled. "I felt something when I saw Ava. It's not like I grabbed some random woman from the grocery store. I didn't have time to figure out what I was going to do about it, and her dad was dying. It wasn't like I could save him right in front of her and claim he miraculously recovered."

I needed time with her, and I got it. But it could come at a cost. The sense that we belonged together refused to leave me. I had to hang on to that and keep trying to win her over.

"Venus agreed to stay here for a while," I said. "She doesn't want to answer to her brothers or either council any more than I do."

Penn's introspective gaze swiveled back to the house like he was hoping to catch a glimpse of her. "She's not pissed?"

I shrugged. "Seemed more upset that rumors got ahead of her. I didn't think she dreaded our union as much as me."

Penn's tone was droll. "I didn't get that impression at all when you two were waiting until the final bell tolled before you did the deed."

Years ago, Venus and I had agreed to wait until right before my birthday, which was almost a month before hers. I hadn't told anyone. When the council asked why we hadn't mated yet, I told them we had time. I had falsely insinuated Venus wanted to wait. Had she been doing the same thing on her end?

"The council's going to be pissed. Simon's vein throbs in his head every time he mentions that you're still single."

"Then they shouldn't have decided for us when Venus and I were just kids." Or they should've made me swear on it. Instead, they gambled. Bet on the odds that I would do the right thing like I always did. They didn't realize I was willing to do a bad thing when I met the person I wanted to spend my life with.

"You put Venus in a shitty position," Penn said. Rare anger rippled under his skin.

My youngest brother was only twenty-five. He was the kid brother who got to do what he wanted. As long as Steel and I were around, Penn didn't have to worry about the tougher aspects of being born into the top family of all shifters. He was smart as hell and supported himself, but he lived a rather carefree life. But he'd always been moodier when Venus was around. She had that effect on people.

"I did, but she has a little time. What if she finds someone she'd rather be with than me?"

"In a month?" Steel shook his head. "What a cluster-fuck. Look, we'll stay here, help in any way we can. Hang out with her dad, run interference with Venus, whatever. Just win Ava over and save us a whopper of a problem."

It'd help to have them under the same roof. They lived in town, but I didn't have much time and I had to juggle Venus and Dorian. Neither was exactly on my side, but I trusted my brothers to help me at any hour of the day.

I went from an empty house to a house full of my family, my formerly contracted mate, and the woman I had to win over by the end of next week. A difficult task now seemed suddenly impossible.

~

AVA

THE WALL of heat wrapped around me before I heard Deacon make a sound. I tossed some fish guts into the pile Dad was making.

"Did you ditch your fiancée and your brothers already?" I asked sweetly.

When I stomped to the backyard and set up my station next to Dad, I gave him a brief rundown minus the talk of other species. I told him Deacon and Venus had agreed they'd marry, neither was thrilled about it, and Venus had heard rumors about me. When he'd been trying to puzzle that together, I told him Deacon's brothers were here. Since Steel was the one who took care of the boat, Dad looked forward to thanking him.

"My brothers are going to hang out with us for a while too," Deacon said. "It's turned into quite a gathering."

Dad paused over his fish. "Do you need the space? I can set up a tent, or find a room in town."

"I won't hear of it, Dorian. I have plenty of space."

I grabbed another silver walleye. I hated gutting fish. This was what my anger toward Deacon drove me to. Dad and I had an agreement. Every time we went fishing, I would happily camp and cast without complaint and catch as many fish as possible, and he'd clean them all. I did the cooking just because he usually paid for everything and I wanted to contribute without stuffing my fingers in guts.

"We can find a room." It didn't make sense to stay here. Dad and I were passing through. "I'm not family. And I'm not your fiancée." I gave him a pointed look.

"You're everything, Ava," he murmured with no hint of tease in his voice.

I paused, the knife hovering over the fish. Dad even stopped and stared at Deacon. I didn't know what to say. A glow sparked in my chest and threatened to expand until I became one of the stars that dotted the night sky.

I had to do something, or I was going to preen. I didn't do that anymore, and I certainly wasn't going to do it when the insides of a walleye covered my hands. I set the knife down with the handle pointing toward Deacon.

"I'm everything but a fish cleaner."

His intense expression softened as he laughed, but I spun away. I rinsed my hands off at the outdoor sink, grateful he had both soap and a towel.

I was about to walk to the house when I stopped. The place wasn't empty. Venus and Deacon's brothers were in there. They were all supposedly dragon shifters. Would I be more like a lamb heading in for the slaughter?

"You're welcome to stay out here with us." Deacon worked so quickly with a knife, I couldn't believe he didn't cut himself.

Dad tossed the innards of the fish he was working on into the pile. "Ava and I can find a motel. I don't want her to be uncomfortable." He must've noticed my discomfort being in the house with the others.

Deacon stopped and set the knife down. He pressed his fingertips into the table and leaned forward. The move wasn't menacing, but more earnest, like he really needed Dad to believe what he said. "I will do everything in my power to make sure Ava is comfortable here. The same goes for you. You are my guests. The others are... a part of my life, however annoying. I swear to you both that you are welcome here."

Power resonated from his words and vibrated deep into my bones. It was like he swore an oath to the universe. He didn't say the words *I swear* or *I promise*, but the intent was there.

Dad must've felt it too. He dipped his head, then raised his gaze to meet mine. "Are you okay with that?"

No, I wasn't. The reality of my oath was sinking in. Did I speak my intention to the universe like him? If there was so much power, so much feeling, in an oath, then what were the consequences?

That wasn't the only reality sinking in. Deacon claimed he didn't want to marry Venus. He argued he liked me, that he wanted to spend the rest of his life with me. And I had tried not to get my hopes up. Then Venus arrived. A tall, gorgeous blonde with ten times the looks of the woman that Chance cheated on me with.

No, I didn't want Chance anymore. But there'd been a time I was willing to uproot my life for him, and I had. Was I willing to toss the possibility that there was something between me and Deacon because of Chance? Wouldn't that mean I was still giving Chance too much say over my life?

I was tired of giving other people power over my future. I had reconciled with myself that I would stay with Deacon for the rest of this camping trip. Dammit, that was what I was going to do. "We'll stay. Do your brothers or Venus need to borrow one of our tents?"

My confidence nearly wavered until a broad grin spread over Deacon's face. "I don't know, but I can't wait to ask them."

CHAPTER

TEN

AVA COULDN'T BELIEVE that I didn't think our catch of walleye would be enough to feed the group. Our kind liked fish, loved it even, but unless we were pulling out something the size of a marlin, feeding four full-grown shifters wouldn't happen. I added several steaks to the pile beside the grill.

Ava sat with her dad on the porch swing I kept on the back patio. I had seen it at the local department store last year and imagined myself sitting on it with my mate watching the sunset. It had been a long year, and as the days ticked by, I thought it had been a foolishly optimistic purchase. I didn't know if Venus was a porch swing girl, but I couldn't picture us enjoying a quiet night side by side.

The picture was crystal fucking clear with Ava.

My brothers hovered around me, keeping a close eye on the food. With dragon shifters, there were always too many cooks in the kitchen. We took our food seriously.

Steel inched closer. I thought he was going to give me a hard time about cooking the ribeye too long, but he spoke too low for any human to hear. "There's been some trouble with a feral."

I held in my groan. Couldn't I take a few days off without things going to hell? "Mountain lion or wolf?" There was a small pack of wolf shifters in the area. I rarely had to deal with them. With so few natural wolves in this region, they had to work nearly as hard as us to be seen. Mountain lions were a different story. All over the state, there were increasing mountain lion sightings. It emboldened some of the more rebellious shifters, the ones who didn't believe dragon shifter authority extended to them.

And sometimes cats were just plain pissy.

"What's going on?" I flipped a steak before Steel made a comment about burning his precious meat.

Penn was the one who answered. "There's been several reports of missing dogs and cats. Then a couple of days ago, there was talk in Wildrose about a farmer who lost a couple head of cattle. Only one carcass was found, all torn up and bloodied. But last night there was a 9-1-1 call."

"Shit." Each type of shifter dealt with their own issues, but if they couldn't contain it from spreading into the human world, dragons got involved.

Steel's expression was grim. "A woman on one of the bike paths with two little kids claimed she was getting stalked by a mountain lion."

My hand tightened around the spatula I held. The

metal warped under my grip. I pried each finger loose. "Do we know who it is?"

"The council wants you to talk with the Catamount pack." Steel shook his head. "I argued I could do it. I have a good relationship with Catamount. But since humans are involved, they think it's best for you to take the lead."

To deal with the problem, I'd have to travel to Catamount pack. They were just across the Canadian border, so I'd have to do it in shifter form.

I didn't want to waste my precious time with Ava, but a feral put us all in danger.

The sliding door opened, and Venus strolled out. She carried a large serving bowl in her hands. "Just in case you thought leaves were only for plants and trees, I made a salad."

"A salad?" Steel's scandalized tone coaxed a smile out of me during a tense situation. "We're not rabbit shift—" His gaze jumped to Ava and her dad. "We're not rabbits."

Penn took a swig out of his metallic water bottle. He was a runner and carted his water with him everywhere. "Did you know that there are at least twelve different edges leaves can have? Serrated like the knife. Doubly serrated. Ciliated means it's fringed like it has tiny hairs. And then leaves themselves have different names—fronds, lycophytes—"

"I don't think we want a lesson, professor," Steel groaned.

"I'm not a professor. Technically, I'm an adjunct instructor until—"

"If you'll excuse me." Venus dumped the bowl on the table. The look she gave him could shrivel all of our balls. "Enjoy your serrated fronds."

"Oh, those are actually—"

Steel elbowed him. "No one cares. We're not eating it anyway."

"I will," Penn said. "And I'm sure Deacon's guests will."

Ava smiled and got off the swing. "It looks delicious." She peered into the bowl while looping her hair behind her ears. "Oh, wow. Those tomatoes are so red. And the romaine looks as fresh as if you just pulled it out of the garden."

Pride replaced the defensiveness that Penn's leaf lecture put in Venus's expression. "I picked the romaine this morning. I have a countertop garden. I usually grow my own tomatoes and cucumbers or buy them at the farmers' market. But these are store bought until those open again."

Ava's eyes brightened. "Oh, yeah? I wasn't able to make it to the farmers' market in Minneapolis." Her smile turned sheepish. "My ex never—" She waved her hand. "I just never made it to the market like I wanted to."

"He would've been your ex faster if you told him you're going to the farmers' market and if he has an issue with that you would bash his head in with a ten-pound butternut squash." Her grin was all vapid innocence.

What the hell, Venus? I agreed with her, but I didn't know how Ava was going to take what she said.

A giggle bubbled from between Ava's lips, and laughter shook Dorian's shoulders as he enjoyed the gentle sway of the swing.

Steel snatched the spatula from my grip to rescue the steaks he must've thought were getting too far beyond rare. "If the ex was a real male, he'd catch the squash, scrape the seeds out, add some butter and salt, and cook it up for you, after he sincerely apologized for being an ass."

We all stared at him, the brother who grudgingly waved some heat around his meat and called it cooked, but apparently knew how to cook a squash.

After the steaks were rescued, Steel noticed everyone's focus on him. His gaze landed on Ava. "That is, if your ex deserved Venus's retaliation."

"He deserved to have his hands tied behind his back and a ten-pound squash slammed into his nut sack." Her tone was granite.

"I can make that happen." Ava would think I was joking, but my offer was serious.

She shrugged it off. "I'm not giving him any more of my energy."

Penn wandered over to the salad and plucked a chunk of tomato out. He popped it into his mouth and chewed.

Venus put her hands on her hips. "We're not animals; we can wait to eat."

"I'm all animal," Penn drawled with a suggestive glint in his eye.

Venus acted like he hadn't said a thing and found a place to sit.

I shouldn't be surprised Penn had a thing for Venus. He was almost ten years younger than her and she had been meant to be my mate. Had he hidden how he felt?

I shoved it from my brain. The only way I could give Penn a chance to see if Venus was into younger males was to get my mate to agree to claim me.

AVA

. . .

LUNCH WENT SURPRISINGLY WELL. But the afternoon took a turn I didn't expect. Deacon had to go to work. It must've been about whatever he and his brothers were discussing when he was cooking the meat. When I had looked back at them, I could see their lips move. It wasn't that loud outside, just some birds chirping and the buzz of bugs, but there was no way I could hear what they were saying.

The differences between me and them didn't seem major. They ate what I ate, if heavy on the carnivore side. Deacon, Steel, Penn, and Venus were all prime physical specimens, but so were millions of other people in the world. Deacon lived in a nice house, he used a fishing pole instead of turning into a creature with teeth and claws to catch his fish, and he was willing to watch Marvel movies. But I'd noticed enough things that are different.

When Deacon was standing around his brothers, they talked so low I doubted I could hear them if I had stood among their little trio. Their hearing was crazy good, they all talked like they lived in the same world, and that was what convinced me the most. It was easy to believe one person was delusional. I even considered the possibility Silver Lake had a cult, but Venus lived in Jade Hills. And they abided by all the same rules they'd grown up with. Like it was natural, not drilled into their brains in order to override common sense.

Venus was chatting with Dad about what he did for a living, what Devils Lake was like, and where his favorite places to camp were. She listened to him, nodding and smiling. When he asked what she did for a living, she said she was a stylist.

A dragon shifter that did hair.

How did these two worlds go together? How did Deacon grill and fish and laugh with his brothers and then heal my dad with nothing but good intentions? My head hurt. I was trying to deny what I'd seen and what I'd heard because I hadn't seen or heard a lot.

I ducked into the bedroom I was using and closed the door. I called Avril. I wanted to tell her everything, but I couldn't. She'd call Dad, concerned about my mental state. But I could tell her enough.

"I was just thinking about you," Avril answered. "I miss our weekly coffee."

Did Deacon drink coffee? Silver Lake had to have a coffee shop. I didn't have a daily caffeine habit, but I was addicted to the socializing. Meeting up with Avril at least once a week got me through my move to the city and the downfall of my relationship.

"I miss it too." If I didn't go back to Minneapolis, I would miss them altogether. How often would I be able to see my best friend?

"How's camping?"

Her question dragged me back to reality. Just yesterday, I was thinking that I needed to talk to Avril about moving in with her, and now I wasn't sure I was going back to Minneapolis. "Yeah, camping... some weird things have happened."

"You met some rugged mountain man, and he squirreled you away, promising you the best sex of your life forever."

I choked. Her guess was terribly accurate. "Funny thing, sort of."

"Whoa, tell me everything." Her voice was full of humor, so part of her thought I was joking.

"Dad collapsed on the boat, I crashed the boat to shore, and this guy and his brother rescued him. At the hospital, the guy, his name is Deacon, came on to me really strong. He gets along really well with Dad, and he insisted on camping with us, so long story short, we're staying in his cabin for the rest of the week. Part of next week too. And he's basically proposed." I squeezed my eyes shut. My story sounded like I had an excellent dream and woke up thinking it was real, and that I decided just to go with it instead of facing the truth.

"Are you serious?" Her tone rose to a high pitch by the end of the question.

"I am, yeah. I can put Dad on if you think I'm lying. But get this," —because what I said wasn't wild enough — "Deacon was sort of already in an arranged marriage, and she's here too. But I think she might be kinda cool."

All I heard on the other end was her breathing. "Are you sure you're okay?"

A light sparked behind my eyes. Irritation. "Does it sound that ridiculous a guy would look at me and want me like that?"

"No," she answered quickly. "No, not at all. You're the type of girl most men walk all over because they're selfish and don't realize what a damn treasure you are. Men with that much good sense aren't common."

I rubbed a hand over my face. "Not the men we've been dating."

"Maybe all the good ones are already in arranged marriages."

I giggled. "You should see her. She is stunning. What does he want with me?"

Avril was earnest when she said, "Don't think like that, Ava. Don't let my surprise strengthen your doubts."

"Thank you, but I'm serious. They act like brother and sister around each other, that's the only thing I can figure out. But I just can't help feeling that I don't have the rest of the story. This stuff doesn't happen." *Not to me.*

"Sometimes it does. But your safety is a priority. Why don't you tell me where you're at? In case you and your dad fall off the face of the earth, I can find you."

I gave her the address and general directions for how to get here. Then I turned the conversation to her to give myself some sense of normalcy. "How are things going with Ian?"

She was quiet for a moment too long before she said, "Fine."

"Oh, what happened?"

"It's nothing. I'm just being overly sensitive."

I doubted it. I tried to give Ian a chance, but when he was around, I couldn't shake the feeling that his persona was fake. After what happened with Chance, thinking about Ian was eye opening. Chance dabbled in narcissism, but Ian was a triple black belt.

"Tell me anyway."

"He did that thing, you know, where he gets down on one knee and I get all excited that he's going to propose, and it turns out he's asking some dumb question instead."

"That's a dick move." A kneeling Ian would be the perfect height to slam my knee to his face. But I doubted that was what Avril did.

"No, it's me. I shouldn't expect him to propose. We got a good laugh out of it."

"The laugh was at your expense."

"It's fine. His buddy recorded it, and he got a lot of hits. Maybe we'll see some money out of the deal."

That asshole. If Ian got enough views to earn some money, he wouldn't share a penny with Avril. She funded most of their relationship.

But she was not in a place to receive critiques about her relationship. I had told her my hesitancy about Ian over the last few years, and she had done the same about Chance. I didn't want to see my friend hurt, but I was afraid of what it would take to get her to leave him.

"I happen to be homeless at the moment. When I get back to town, do you think you'd mind tolerating a roommate?" I rushed on. "It'd only be for a few weeks. Just until I find a job and a place I can afford."

I'd be lucky if it only took a few weeks, but I didn't want to sound any more desperate than I was.

"Absolutely, Ava. You never have to ask."

I hated to revisit the topic of her jackass boyfriend. "Ian might have a problem with it."

"He won't. I have an entire lower level in my condo that's only used for his guitar and recording equipment." Avril chuckled. I was close enough with her to hear how forced her laughter was. Technically, Ian didn't live with her. Her place had more space than the two-bedroom flat he shared with his high school buddy. Ian shouldn't have a say at all about what Avril did with her condo. She earned twice as much as him while he tried to get his influencer career off the ground.

I would never tell Avril that though. Chance was looking like a catch compared to Ian. No wonder I had stayed with him too long. I should send him a thank-you letter for breaking up with me.

Shitty timing though. I would've liked to have kept my job while trying to find a new place to live.

There was a loud knock on my door. I jumped and let out a yelp.

"Is everything okay? Is the hot guy going to eat you alive and not in the good way?"

Venus called from the other side of the door, "Human, come outside with me. I have to show you something."

The command in her voice nearly made me drop the phone and jump to attention.

I told my heart rate to calm down. "It's Deacon's fiancée. Ex-fiancée? She wants to talk to me." She wanted to show me something. That sounded ominous.

"Don't get murdered."

I said "I won't" automatically when I had zero evidence to back up my confidence. Venus didn't have to be a shifter for me to know that I wouldn't stand a chance against her.

ELEVEN

D eacon

I ENTERED city hall behind my brothers. What I really wanted to do was slam the door behind them and sprint to my pickup. Ava was at my place, alone with Venus. Dorian was there, but I didn't know what chance he would stand if Venus decided to be wicked. They could chitchat for an hour, but I'd seen Venus verbally slay a man until he physically bled. It was a nosebleed, but it still counted.

She wasn't her parents, but she was raised by them. She and her brothers seemed to lack the cruelty of their parents, but the rest of us were on guard. Jade clan was fairly reclusive. We didn't really know them.

I had to table my concern about her for the moment. The four members of Silver Lake's city council were gathered in the meeting room. The council consisted of elders.

Even though our kind had a human lifespan, we still valued experience.

I was "voted" mayor as soon as my parents died. That was how we blended our clan leadership to look like we were human. But the minimum age requirement for the council was forty-five. They had passed the milestone age of thirty-five and were securely mated. Their moods were more stable, and they'd seen enough of our kind's consequences carried out to have a heavy respect for our traditions.

My brothers took their seats toward the end of the long rectangle table, on either side of the head of the table. I sat at the head and glanced at everyone present.

Orla was the oldest member. She was approaching her eightieth birthday, but she still hit up happy hour at the golf course's country club and was known for preferring more whiskey than Coke in her drinks. Across from her was Simon. He just retired from his landscaping business last year and agreed to sit on the council when his predecessor passed away. Both Orla and Simon were even-tempered and practical. They weren't below requiring me to mate with Venus or face the consequences of not being mated by my birthday.

The idea to mate me with someone from Jade clan came from Deborah's mother. Her mother had passed. Deborah was forty-six and had been hitting on me since I turned eighteen. I'd been saying no since I was eighteen. Supporting the Silver and Jade clan union was fifty-eight-year-old Bronson. His first had passed away, and the rumor was that he was dating a male from Jade Hill, and he'd rather have enforced peace between our clans than deal with any opposition himself.

Deborah's pleased gaze was on me. "I hear Venus is in town."

"She is." I wasn't giving Deborah the satisfaction of having control over my personal life. I certainly wasn't telling her about Ava. "What's this about a feral mountain lion shifter?"

Deborah's gaze turned shrewd. She might have a thing for young males, but she wasn't an idiot. She knew I was hiding something.

Orla answered as if she didn't sense the tension circling me. "It's the council's recommendation to put a kill order on the feral shifter. He's already tried to attack humans. It's only a matter of time before he succeeds. If a game warden gets to him first, you can imagine the trouble it'd cause in several areas."

Like when the feral shifted back to his human form after death. Yeah, that'd be an issue.

As if that wasn't enough of a concern, the family's pride was. They might not be willing to do anything about their feral member, but if humans dealt with it, they'd rally against them.

One of the worst parts of my position was having the authority to order the end of another shifter's life. The absolute worst part was when I had to carry out the job myself. One of the requirements of the mayor was to be involved in the kill. That way, we wouldn't sit at the head of the table and arbitrarily issue the order. In rare instances, other members of the ruling family could carry out the kill, but I wouldn't ask that of my brothers.

If I turned thirty-five with no mate, they'd be facing the task soon enough.

"It is ordered." I held in my groan. That meant I would have to be gone from home longer than I planned.

This wasn't a job I could put off until next week. The mountain lion shifter could be stalking a hiker, or worse, another child.

I looked at each brother. "May I request your help?" It would go faster.

Steel nodded as if he had expected to accompany me. Penn dipped his head, but he looked as unhappy as me about the task.

"If there's nothing else?"

I was nearly out of the chair before Deborah spoke. "When can we expect the mating between you and Venus to occur? There should be a celebration."

Bronson nodded. "Have we cleared it with Jade clan to have the ceremony here?"

"We don't need to contact Jade about the mating ceremony." I wouldn't lie to my council. But right now, the truth would require too much explanation. These people would interfere and scare Ava away for good.

"I disagree," Bronson said. "A big reason behind this arrangement is to open communication between our clan and theirs."

"A big reason behind this arrangement was that no one wanted to confront Jade's mayor about their heavy-handed enforcement and the sheer cruelty they used to rule over their people." Silver's council had thought to gain backdoor support by uniting us. Jade's council had thought they'd gain backdoor access to Silver's power structure if their daughter was mated to the leader. Thirty years since the pact had been made, and the council had different people and both leaders had changed. The next generation was stuck with the reper-cussions.

Orla folded her hands on top of the table. "I can

justify what we did all those years ago, but I realize now how it impacted you. Still, Deacon, you are cutting your mating terribly close. I know you realize you aren't given the same grace period other shifters are when they are still single at thirty-five."

Simon added, "It seems that instead of trying to unite our clans, both you and Venus are stalling until the last minute. It seems you and Venus are cut from the same cloth. So why the delay?"

It was because Venus and I were so much alike there was nothing between us.

"As soon as Venus and I have news to pass along, you'll be the first to know." Aside from my brothers, but that was a given. "It's not my birthday yet."

I rose, indicating the meeting was over. Steel stood next. Then Penn. We walked out as a unit, a not-so-subtle dig at the council. I might be the leader of Silver clan, but they wouldn't quit trying to be the real power behind the throne.

"Anyone have to stop anywhere first?" We didn't need weapons to hunt. We dealt with other shifters naturally.

"I just want to get this done as fast as possible," Steel grumbled. Penn nodded.

"Let's go hunt a feral."

And then I'd clean all the blood off me and hope that I could face Ava without terrifying her.

～

AVA

.   .   .

I STUMBLED THROUGH THE TREES. Long grasses tangled around my ankles. Wasn't there a trail we could use? Venus strode through the underbrush like it was a polished marble floor.

I told Dad we were going for a hike. The farther we got away from Deacon's house, the more I thought I should've told him to call the police if I didn't return in a couple hours. Or if Venus returned without me.

"Where did you say we were going again?"

Without looking back, Venus said, "I didn't tell you the first time."

Fear made me stop. There was no telling how much poison ivy I had walked through. Or did they have poison birch here? Poison oak? Regardless, if there were leaves of three, I didn't have the wherewithal to let them be. I was probably covered in itchy plant oil and ticks. The sensation of creepy-crawlies erupted over my body.

"I'm going back." I turned around and branches tangled in my hair. These woods were not meant to walk through. The trees were a mix of deciduous varieties and shrubs. The mixture made sure that there were branches sticking out at every height. I had scratches across my face, over my arms, and down my legs. I hadn't put pants on when Venus asked me to follow her. I didn't think she had to show me something a mile away from the cabin.

"We're almost there, human."

"It doesn't matter. I'm done." I took a few steps, and a hand gripped my shoulder. I yelped and whirled around. Venus towered over me. "How did you move that fast?"

She cocked her brow as if she couldn't believe I'd have to ask. She sighed and rolled her eyes to the sky. "Fine, I'll show you here, but if I lose a scale thanks to these branches, I'm blaming you."

"What are you talking about?"

Venus's expression changed. She was no longer haughty, or defensive, or annoyed. She was dead serious, only I worried she was serious and I was dead. Goose bumps prickled my skin.

"Get the fear out now, human. I'm going to show you what we really are." She ripped her shirt off over her head. I had all sorts of monstrous images running through my mind, but a voluptuous woman wasn't one of them. "Time is running out, and you need to know." She dropped her shorts and underwear and stepped out of them, kicking her shoes off at the same time. "Whether or not you think so, what you see in a minute is going to be the biggest decision maker."

It was like a hologram at first. I questioned what I was really seeing. Her cheekbones sharpened and the bones in her temples grew prominent. She was a tall person, but my head tipped back as she grew even bigger. Then her skin changed. Where there was creamy bronze flesh before, a metallic-green sheen covered her.

And then she really started to change.

My gasp was lost in the cracking of the branches as Venus grew and shifted into a magical creature I'd only seen in books.

The creature's back didn't breach the treetops, but she was easily three or four times my size. And she had scales. Gorgeous shimmering scales.

A giant tail that sloped off her back twitched. When I dragged my gaze to meet eyes the same color as Venus's, I gasped. There was intelligence in those eyes. It was her. Venus looked back at me from within a fantastical creature. I backed up, tripping on the underbrush. I toppled backward, gathering more gouges and scratches as I went.

Now the dragon really towered over me. Fascination morphed into terror when Venus opened her mouth. A long snout that housed sharp pointed teeth gaped over me. My mind had held strong until this point.

"No." I scrambled backward. The flesh in my palms tore open.

The rumble that came from the beast didn't sound exactly like a lion's roar. It was a foreign sound that sent fear straight into my heart.

I shouted and flipped around to all fours, then took off like I was in the track race of my life.

The ground shook under me as heavy footstep after heavy footstep landed behind me. Oh, god, she was chasing me.

My hair tore as it snagged branches. I got whacked in the face and across my torso. But I didn't stop.

She could have easily caught me. I was logical enough to know that. Was she playing with me like I was nothing more than a little field mouse? Was the deep rumble coming from her nothing but maniacal laughter? I wasn't sticking around to find out.

When I walked into these trees with Venus, I wouldn't have admitted I didn't fully believe the whole dragon shifter thing. I had no doubts now, but that didn't make it better. That made it so much worse.

Up ahead, I could see Deacon's house. Would Venus let me get that far? She might not want to mate Deacon, but I was still a complication in her mind.

All I wanted to do was get to the house, grab Dad, and jump into the pickup. I wanted this house and these people in our rearview mirror.

As the trees thinned, I sped up. My legs burned, and so did my lungs, but I didn't care. I was almost there.

"Ava!" Venus called behind me.

Did she have to change back to yell my name?

I didn't care. I was so close to freedom, I wasn't stopping.

A large shadow moved into my path. I didn't have time to stop. I barreled into Deacon and he caught me around the upper arms.

"For fuck's sake, Venus. What the hell are you doing?"

I didn't realize tears were streaming down my face until I stared up at him and drew in a shaky breath. But I didn't register his concerned look or his broad shoulders or how safe I felt around him.

Blood. He was covered. His clothes were clean, and it looked like he had tried to wipe his face off. But blood splattered his neck and his forearms. And his hands where they gripped my shoulders.

I jerked out of his grip. Did he take his clothes off like Venus and shift? How did he get blood all over him? Is it his or someone else's?

All the emotions fueling my run exploded. I opened my mouth, ready to scream until my world was back to normal.

TWELVE

eacon

I CLAMPED a hand over her mouth. "You can't scream." Her face turned red as a high-pitched squealing noise emitted from her throat.

"You're going to worry your dad." I was crushing her body against me so she couldn't run anywhere. When she realized she couldn't free herself, she savagely shook her head. I had to let go, worried she'd break her own neck.

"That doesn't make me feel any better!" She continued trying to shove away from me. "Don't touch me. You're covered in blood."

Was that what made her scream? I had forgotten that I wasn't fully cleaned up. She was terrified before she charged into me. How must she feel now? "Do you promise not to run?"

The look she gave me said *how dare you ask me to promise something after the last oath I made?*

"Look, if you run, I will catch you. If you want to keep your dad out of this, you need to listen to me."

My words got through to her. She relaxed and finally nodded. I took my hand off her mouth. I had washed my hands and face off the best I could, but it wasn't perfect. I'd hate to get another male's blood on her. She wouldn't handle the truth behind it well.

I looked over her shoulder. Venus had her hands propped on her bare hips. She was completely naked. Either she tried to have sex with my mate, or she shifted. Since I hadn't known Venus to go after females, I guessed it was the latter.

"Why the hell did you do that?"

Venus shrugged, her generous breasts jiggling. Nudity was more accepted among my kind. I had no problem looking her in the eyes.

"She had to see her first shift, Deacon. You couldn't keep putting it off. You're running out of time, and both our clans are going to suffer the fallout. You know how the first shift makes or breaks humans."

"Well, you fucking broke her."

"I thought she was going to kill me. She was all growly and—" Ava glanced over her shoulder and started. "She's naked."

Ava's gaze darted around her as she avoided looking at me and Venus. Was she more unsettled about the nudity?

"Shifters aren't as scandalized by naked people," I said. "Technically, it's our natural state. We can't shift with clothing on."

Ava held her hands up and closed her eyes. "This has been *a day*. I believe in shifters, okay? And maybe I could even get used to them, but I don't think I'll ever like her towering over me and baring her teeth."

I rolled my eyes to Venus. "Seriously?"

"Get pissy all you want, Deacon, but I did what you were too afraid to do." She spun around and stomped back into the trees, her ass cheeks jiggling, but the only female I wanted to look at was my mate.

"I'm sorry," I said softly.

She grudgingly lifted her gaze to mine, then winced. "Why are you covered in blood?"

I let out a heavy exhale. I hated how right Venus was. I could deny it all I wanted, but she had done what I'd been putting off. I had hoped to win over Ava sooner, or to be mated to her so it didn't matter. She would be mine and couldn't leave me. But my hesitance had hurt her.

Telling her the truth could sever what ties we had built between us. It didn't matter. If she was my mate, if this pull between us was real, the truth wouldn't frighten her away. "We have rules in our society. We do our best to live according to human laws, but there are parts of our nature that we can't escape."

She dragged her gaze back to me. She was tense again, but she was listening.

"We're all pack creatures. Dragons have clans. Wolves and mountain lions have packs, same with bears. You get the picture." When she nodded, I continued. "We aren't allowed to be alone. We might shift into other creatures, but we aren't other creatures. We're shifters. Although we spend most of our time as humans, we can be extremely aggressive. Since we spend most of our time in this form, following rules, getting told what to do, it can leave little outlet for that aggression. We're no longer at war. We're no longer getting killed off regularly."

She folded her arms across her chest and lifted her chin like she didn't want to empathize with what I was saying, but she did. "It's kind of like humans, in a way. Our emotions need an outlet no matter how many generations of our ancestors have sat behind a desk."

"Exactly. But we don't have therapists. We can't just go to the gym for a hard workout. The aggression builds. When we're alone, there is no family to recognize the signs. No friends to spar or wrestle with, no outlet. Shifters get dangerous. We call it feral."

Her gaze brushed over my neck and my forearms. She was looking at the blood splatter. "And I guess you don't give them a stern talking to?"

"After a certain point, there is no reasoning. A mountain line shifter was trying to attack kids. If we waited much longer to deal with him, then he might've killed one. If a game warden got to him first—we don't stay in shifter form after we're dead. You can surmise the complications of having a human witness that."

Her brows pinched together. She opened her mouth, then snapped it closed. Finally, she cleared her throat. "You killed someone?"

My voice was heavy when I answered. "It's my duty as mayor. And it's a duty I wouldn't wish on anyone else."

I closed my eyes and rubbed my temples. The beginnings of a headache were coming on. Shifters healed quickly, but that didn't stop the stress of the memories from adding pressure to my brain.

"Oh, Deacon. I'm sorry."

My eyelids flew open to meet her gaze. "You are?"

"It's obvious it bothers you." She shook her head, her expression sad. "Is it like dementia? The shifter wouldn't think of doing anything to hurt a child before he was..."

"Feral?"

She nodded. She switched her folded arms to hug herself. "Sounds like it's awful for all involved."

"It is. But we fight in our shifter forms. We aren't allowed to use weapons unless there's a dire need to stay hidden from humans. It's one reason why we live in such rural areas."

She looked past me and waved. I glanced over my shoulder. Dorian was out on the patio. I doubt he'd seen a naked Venus, but he also shouldn't see me. "I can't walk past your dad like this. There is a clearing in the trees with a small stream. I'm sure that's where Venus shifted?"

Color leeched from Ava's face, but she didn't otherwise react. "No. I got impatient and was going to come back when she..." She waved a hand in the air and her tone was stilted when she said, "Shifted."

So Venus shifted in the trees and added the ability to slam into a trunk and topple a tree over to all the ways she could terrify Ava? Figured. "It's a beautiful place. I'll have to show you sometime."

"How about now?"

I stared at her for a moment. Did she invite herself along? Just in case I heard correctly, I said, "Sure."

She called over my shoulder, "Dad, I'm going for another hike with Deacon."

Her dad hollered back. "I'll start fixing supper for all of us!"

Shyness entered her expression. "Can I see what you, um, what you look like when you shift?"

I might end up doing what I never thought I'd do and thank Venus for what she did.

~

AVA

WE DIDN'T PASS Venus while we were following the trail back into the trees.

"Can you fly?" I briefly closed my eyes. Never in my life did I think I would be asking someone if they could fly. But last week, I didn't know dragons were real.

"We can, but we don't. Too risky."

He walked so effortlessly beside me. I was picking through the grass and stepping over bent and decaying tree limbs. He held his hand out for me to grab as I maneuvered every obstacle. He was back to being thoughtful Deacon, and even more disturbing, I no longer noticed the blood.

"So what happens if you fly? What are the consequences?"

He grasped my hand and tugged me to a stop. I had the sense he was going to tell me something else about his kind that I wouldn't like.

Frowning, he inspected my hands and arms. They'd taken the brunt of the branches. "I can heal you."

I liked his concern. What did that say about me? "They're all superficial. They sting, but it's no big deal. Will I pass out for an entire day?"

"I don't know. Your father was the first one I've

shared the gift with. I'm not around a lot of humans, and they're all healthy when we interact."

"I'm fine. Don't worry about it. Really."

He dipped his head in acknowledgment and slipped my hand back into his. "Back to your earlier question, we can't really do shifter jails. We have limited punishments and consequences. Otherwise, humans would wonder why Silver Lake's jail cells are the size of gymnasiums. They'd have questions about the lead-lined walls. Even the smaller cells for the other shifters would still look like a zoo if a human walked through. We can't stop someone from shifting."

He was telling me the answer without telling me the answer. "You kill them."

His nod was grim. "In the old days, it was different. Dragons commanded the earth and the sky. Shifters could shift, no matter who was watching. But when humans became the dominant population, things had to change."

I couldn't believe we were talking about the same planet. "When would that have been? I get there were no dragon bones for archaeologists to find since you change back after death. But hasn't anyone accidentally seen a dragon, or even a mountain lion midshift? I feel like the secret would've gotten out by now."

He started walking again but didn't let go of my hand. "We have a few gifted shifters who can help block memories in humans. Steel is one of those shifters."

"You can heal and Steel can wipe a mind? What's Penn's gift?"

"Being annoyingly smart." He gave me a quick smile. "I'm kidding, but I'm not. Being forced to live rurally and away from larger communities can isolate our abilities.

My parents saw the technology revolution and used it to bring high-level skills back into the clan. Steel is the city police, but he's looking at online law classes for other members of our clan. Getting our kind to be away long enough for undergrad and graduate schooling used to be impossible. They'd be away from the clan too long."

"Is that how Penn's a professor?"

"He'd tell you he's an adjunct instructor, but yes. He's smart as hell and was able to take college classes in high school. He finished his undergrad and grad school in record time. He said he has some classes left to complete his PhD, but he can do it all online—but the big deal is that he can use that knowledge from Silver Lake thanks to the internet. But the ease with which he does it? Yeah, I think it's a unique ability, like my healing. We're a ruling family."

"Can you breathe fire?" That question was way weirder to ask than the flying one.

"My brothers and I can. It's not like flamethrower level. The ruling families have the ability to spit fire, but we don't utilize the skill very much. There are enough wildfires in the world without us exhaling flames into the trees."

Shifters roamed the world before humans populated it. I didn't know world history. I didn't know what dinosaurs came before others, or how long dinosaurs were gone before cavemen evolved into civilization. "Are you saying the reign of shifters was pre-or post-dinosaur?"

The corner of his mouth tipped up. "Post."

It was alarming how it all made sense.

The trickle of water reached my ears. The stream was small, like Deacon said. It was only a few feet wide, but ripples on the surface made it clear which direction it ran. Deacon turned us to follow the flow.

"It forms a small pool up ahead. My brothers and I have stashed some supplies here for times like this."

The reminder that he killed someone sobered me. "Was the reign of shifters brutal?"

"Most likely. We don't really have records."

Any records would've been too dangerous to keep. "So how did humans become dominant? I was afraid of Venus before she turned into a creature that looked like it could eat me in three bites."

He laughed. "Venus is way too picky to eat someone. In those days, shifters didn't reproduce quickly. Long gestations with centuries to decades between births stabilized the population."

"Built-in population control?"

"Population control that we traded when we saw we were outnumbered. By then, the elders were tired. They were world weary and they envied the humans for their blink of a lifespan. So a deal was struck among our more powerful beings."

I stopped. "Are you telling me there were witches and wizards?"

His laughter rang through the trees. "Ava, like us, they are no longer very powerful. But back then, they changed our world."

"I'm surprised all of your people agreed."

He shrugged, and we continued walking. "All of what I'm telling you took a great deal of time. There were definitely wars fought over the decision."

It didn't matter the civilization, you couldn't please everyone.

A glittery blue pool sparkled up ahead. It wasn't large,

but more of an area where the stream widened before it narrowed again.

"It's not that deep."

He released my hand and crossed to a large boulder. "No, and it's colder than hell. But it does the job, so I don't have to bring the job back to my home."

He shoved a large boulder to the side like it weighed no more than a bowling ball. He pulled out a plastic Rubbermaid that was buried underneath.

"You're welcome to take your shoes off and wade. It's refreshing." He opened the bin and withdrew a small plastic bottle and a washcloth. He wiggled the bottle. "Eco-friendly body wash."

Splashing in freshwater sounded lovely after the day I had. I was stepping out of my shoes when Deacon yanked his shirt over his head.

I couldn't quit staring. The broad shoulders I admired underneath his shirt were far better bare. I was caught on his abs when he unbuckled his pants and let them drop.

"What are you doing?" I squeaked.

His grin was unrepentant. "I'm bathing."

He gave me a wink before he waded into the water.

I continued staring at the spot he had been standing in. Did I see what I really saw? He was a large man. That was flaccid?

He kept his back to me as he crouched in the water and began washing the blood off.

"I can feel you looking at me." Humor laced his voice.

I jerked my gaze off of him, but it only lasted a second. His ass was as impressive as the rest of him. It looked as hard as the boulder he moved, but unlike the rock, I could pinch his butt.

He claimed nudity didn't bother his kind. I was tired

of being shocked for the day. I gingerly picked my way over the rocks until my feet were fully submerged in the stream.

"Nice, isn't it?" he asked.

My gaze was back on him when I said, "Yes. It is."

CHAPTER

THIRTEEN

D eacon

AVA COULDN'T KNOW how much I could smell her arousal. I liked the way we talked on the way here, but when her interest roared after I took my shirt off, I fucking loved it.

I ran my soapy hands through my hair and all over my body. Suds flowed into the stream. My brothers and I used the same brand that wouldn't hurt the water. They went home to clean up, knowing that I had extra complications with Venus and two human guests, and that I would need to hurry and return home.

But I'd rather be here with Ava. Her questions gave me hope. The more curious she was about my kind, perhaps the sooner she could accept us.

I couldn't tell the council until she was ready. They would have issues, and so would Jade clan's council. But

Venus hadn't rushed off to tell them. She must have her own reasons to keep quiet.

Once I was fully rinsed off, I picked my way back to the boulder. I returned my body wash and took out the plastic bag full of clothing. I'd have to come back and replenish what I used. I shoved everything else back in the bin and put the bin back in the hole I dug for it. The rock was returned to its spot over the top to keep it from getting blown away or rummaged through by curious animals.

I should get dressed, but Ava had her back to me. I shamelessly enjoyed her awkwardness. She wiggled her toes in the water and then glanced up at me, zooming her gaze quickly away.

I chuckled. She scowled but refused to look at me.

"I saw you take out clean clothes. Why don't you get dressed?"

"Because it's too enjoyable to watch you right now."

"You like making me nervous?"

I moved through the water toward her. I'd seen the way she was picking her steps. The sharp edges of the rocks and pebbles in the water didn't bother me. They could cut her foot open though. "Only for the right reasons."

She jerked her head up like it surprised her I had gotten so close without her noticing. Her golden hair glinted in the shards of sun breaking through the tree canopy.

I swooped her into my arms. She yelped and struggled. I tried not to laugh but failed.

"Hold on." I grinned. "I'll put you down if you want. But I thought I'd carry you to shore so you don't rip your feet open."

This time, she met my gaze with a glare. "You should ask first."

"I'd like to get to a place where you trust me so much I don't need to."

She blinked at me as if she couldn't make out what I said. "I've been in that place before with a man. It didn't work out too well. But I'll accept the lift to shore, thank you."

"I would hope by now you realize I am not that man." I reached the edge of the water and carefully set her down. Even though she shot down my advances, my dick was still at half-mast. I didn't want her to be intimidated by it or feel like I was trying to make her uncomfortable, but I wanted her to get used to me.

"You realize how far fetched that sounds, right?" She whirled around and her gaze dropped to my growing erection. The scent of her arousal deepened. I wouldn't act on it until she invited me to.

"I find nothing about us far fetched."

"We haven't known each other very long. You claim to want to marry me or for me to be your mate, or whatever. And you expect me to take your word on it. You don't know me. You don't know what I like, you don't know what my favorite color is, and you haven't seen a lot of my personality. What if you're around me for a month and you find me aberrant?"

I had to remember humans weren't like dragons. Not only did Ava have to get past the fact that I was a dragon shifter, she had to accept the significance of mating. It wasn't marriage. It wasn't saying vows in front of someone who had a piece of paper on their wall that gave them the approval to hear those vows. It wasn't living together and sharing the same last name until one or both of us decided it wasn't working and we went our separate ways. We traded a lot of our life to live among humans, but the seriousness of mating remained.

Finding someone we wanted to be with wasn't just pointing to a pretty face in the crowd and saying "that one." That was the part she didn't realize. "Shifters don't exactly have fated mates. Yeah, at one time we did. But that was when we had time to search the world high and low. We had centuries to find that perfect someone. It's not like that now, our time is limited. But that doesn't mean we're willing to settle with just anyone."

She folded her arms and cocked a hip out. My manhood decided to find everything she did sexy. My erection throbbed, but I was intent to make her understand. It would have to wait.

"Venus?" she asked.

"That was political. Matings can be arranged for several reasons, but they still have significance, and they're necessary. But when I saw you, I felt it."

Some of the defiance drained out of her. "Felt what?"

"I don't know. I saw you and I wanted you. Yes, it's only been a few days since we've been together, but that feeling hasn't changed, it's only grown stronger." I closed the distance between us, careful to stay far enough away that I didn't poke her with my erection. "Stronger, Ava. I'm getting to know you, and it only makes me want you more. Like, I know you like superhero movies."

She swallowed hard. "Well, obviously."

Frustrating woman. She insisted on talking me out of how I felt as much as herself. "Not just any superhero films, Marvel ones. I would bet you've watched them all in order."

She ran her fingers along her collar but didn't deny that I was right.

"I like your loyalty to your dad. You would probably be fine if you never went fishing again, but you will go whenever your dad wants to. I would even bet that after he's gone, you'll continue to fish just to relive the memories. Just because you know how much he loved it."

Her blue-green eyes misted over, enhancing the green, but she said nothing.

I continued. "You're mad at your ex. And so am I. You want to know why? Because the way he treated you is making it harder for you to trust me. We'll be good together, I know it. You're too afraid to find out that I'm right, and it's all that jackass's fault."

"I gave up everything for him." Her voice cracked, and she sniffled. "I missed spending my mom's last year with her. I didn't plan to move, but he convinced me. And then he always made excuses about why we shouldn't travel back too often." She huffed out of breath, her anger infusing the air around us. "And I listened. I could have spent more time with my mom, but instead I listened to some narcissistic asshole."

I pulled her into my arms. My erection had dwindled in response to her distress and anger, but I wished I would've gotten dressed. I just wanted to hold her and make her feel better. "If only I could go back in time and tell him to fuck off when he first asked you out."

Her laugh was shaky. She planted her hands against my chest and gazed up at me. "You make it really hard to dislike you."

She cupped my face with her hands and rose on her tiptoes. She pressed her lips to mine. It was a perfect moment. She made the first move, a small sign she trusted me.

I let her take the lead until she tentatively licked her tongue against my lips. I opened like she wanted and the beast inside me nearly took over to demand a claiming.

I wouldn't claim her tonight, but maybe I could taste her.

I carried her to the boulder I had moved earlier. It had a gently sloping side that I often used to perch on when I just wanted to think or when I wasn't ready to go back to my house.

I set her down and kneeled in front of her. Her wide eyes were on me. I hooked my fingers around her waistband. "Tell me to stop if you want, but I just want to put my mouth on you."

She steadied herself with her hands behind her on the rock.

She lifted her hips as I rolled her shorts down. I grabbed the shirt from my clean clothing pile and wedged it under her butt.

"Take your shirt off. I want to see all of you."

I thought this would be it. She'd tell me to stop before I got her pants past her feet. But she didn't. I slid her shorts over her sandals and she dragged her shirt off. Her breasts were the most tantalizing creamy round globes I'd ever seen. Every part of her could steal my attention, but the need to have my tongue on her drove me.

I dropped her clothing on top of my clean ones. Then I ran my hands up her legs, over her thighs, and onto her hips.

The smell of sweet Ava surrounded me. She wouldn't need much to get ready, but I wasn't pushing her that far, no matter how much I wanted to.

I brushed my thumb over her mound and the trimmed patch of curls she kept. "Fucking beautiful." My face was so close to her center. All I had to do was lean forward.

I refused to rush this. We had privacy. We had time. I would show her that the pull between us was so much more satisfying when we gave in to our nature.

Her lacy beige bra was still on. I had gotten a glimpse of her underwear. Also beige. I liked her simple tastes. If she wanted to wear flaming-red lingerie, I didn't care. Granny panties? Didn't care.

I rose enough to skim my fingers around her rib cage and unhook her bra.

"I can't believe I'm doing this." Her voice trembled. I sensed her anticipation, but also her nerves.

"I am doing it because I've been dying to touch you since I first saw you."

She flicked her pink tongue over her lower lip. "I don't have—I don't usually—" Red flamed along her cheeks. "I don't have any protection with me."

"We're not going that far, sweet Ava." There was a lot she still didn't know, and I wasn't going to pause to talk about dragon biology. I cupped my hands over her breasts and rolled her pebbled nipples between my thumb and forefinger. "I want to, and we will, but not tonight."

She nodded. Her pupils were dilated, her cheeks still flushed. She looked like a siren I summoned out of the lake.

I came out of my squat enough to press a firm kiss on her lips. She closed her eyes briefly to return it, then watched as I licked and kissed my way down her neck. I stopped at each breast and sucked her dusky-pink nipples into my mouth. She arched into me. I was afraid she'd tumble off the rock, but maybe it was just an excuse to put my hands at her waist.

I couldn't wait any longer. Her scent, so full of promise, so ripe, taunted me. I crouched down, barely keeping from scraping my erection on the hard surface of the rock. I doubt that would've slowed me.

I placed my hands between her thighs and pushed them open as far as they could go without robbing her balance. The quick pants of her breathing echoed in my ears. She was uncomfortable being so open to me.

"Ava, I could look at you like this all day, and lose myself in you all night."

"How do you know the right things to say?"

"Because I'm telling you exactly what I feel." I lowered my head as I gently used my thumbs to spread her lower lips apart.

I licked my tongue through her seam to her clit, circled her swollen nub, and reversed my course.

She bucked her hips, and one foot slipped off the rock. Without looking, I caught her around the ankle and brought her foot to rest on my shoulder.

I found her clit again, and I played. She was closer to release than I thought. A testament to how tightly she reined in her passion. If I wasn't sure how she felt about me before now, I knew. She wanted me. It was the anxiety from her past experience that was keeping us apart.

I took her to the brink and then backed off. A needy moan escaped her. She was hanging her head back. I'd love to see the golden cascade her tresses made, but I was enjoying the view right here just fine.

Her thighs quivered by my ears. I softened my tongue

and slowed my rhythm as I pushed my index finger inside her.

As soon as I was inside, she rocked her hips, riding my finger.

"That's it, Ava. Let go."

I could tease her with an orgasm for hours, but I wanted to give her this release. I wanted to taste it; I wanted to witness it; I wanted to feel it. I covered her with my lips and sucked her little bud until a scream ripped from her throat. It wasn't just any incomprehensible sound she made. It was my name on the wind.

She called out my fucking name.

I drew out her pleasure, thrusting in and out of her and holding steady with my mouth while she wildly rode through her climax.

Her foot slipped off my shoulder, and she lost her grasp with her hands. Ripping myself away, I caught her before she fell. I picked her up and turned us. I sat where she had been and draped her legs over my lap. She was breathing hard against my chest, her head tucked under my chin. She had a hand on my shoulder and I covered it with my own.

"That was... that was..."

I gave her fingers a squeeze. "That was only the beginning."

∼

AVA

EVERY CELL in my body was alive, vibrating with more electricity than I had ever experienced. I was naked. My

132

bra had tumbled to the ground at some point, but I hadn't noticed.

Energy coursed through me. I wasn't usually this invigorated after sex. The insecurities that I'd kept at bay usually returned tenfold once my ex was done. But not right now. With Deacon holding me, and after the things he had said and the way he had looked at me, those insecurities were dormant. I didn't know for how long, and I didn't care.

His hard length pulsed between us. He was a large man. Everywhere. He fascinated me. I'd had a few partners in my life, yet I'd never considered more than a cursory glance at their privates. Whether it was because I hadn't felt bold enough or because I really didn't like the looks of it, it didn't matter. This was different, and that seemed to be the trend with Deacon. Everything was different.

And what I'd seen of his erection was glorious. I wanted a better look.

I shifted a couple of inches away from him to look down.

"It's okay, Ava. This was for you, not me."

I met his hooded gaze. "This is for me too. You have a really nice cock, and I'd like to touch it."

"Touching it might make it go boom." The corner of his mouth curled up. "But far be it from me to deny you your pleasure."

I scooted down his lap. "Oh, ick. I'm getting my—you know—all over you."

"I should hope so. You smell delicious."

He always said the right things, but sometimes I didn't know how to take his words.

"It's even worse now," he grumbled. "I know how

amazing you taste, and all I can think about is when I can put my head between your thighs again."

Even after what we just did, a scandalized gasp escaped from between my lips. Maybe scandalized wasn't the right word. Delighted might be a little closer.

I touched the tip of my finger to the tip of his erection. His cock twitched.

I held in the giggle. It didn't seem appropriate, but it felt natural. That was why everything got so confusing around Deacon. If I tuned into what I was feeling, I would see how comfortable I was around him. The ease of being with him. The way he boosted me up instead of punching me down. It was my mind that was creating the obstacles. I followed my heart once, and it led me to a dead end far from home.

But my mind was blissfully silent right now. I was focused on how his hard shaft felt in my hand. My fingers stroked over hot skin. His approving groan encouraged me to continue.

He didn't pressure me to give him head. He insisted I didn't have to get him off. And that was why I kept going. Because I wanted to.

I pumped up and down his hard length. The crown of his erection glistened, inviting me to swipe my thumb over the tip. His balls were tight. Maybe next time I would cup them while I jerked him off.

Look at me. Planning a next time.

There was no doubt I would like to do this again. Sitting naked together. The scattering of dark hair on his chest soft against my arm. His hard thighs under me. I liked the way his abs clenched as he leaned back to give me room to stroke.

In my grip, he swelled. His body was full of energy so

tightly restrained that if he exploded, it'd take both of us out with it. I'd probably end up on my ass and in some poison ivy, and he'd be back in the water.

He didn't lose control. Even as he gritted his teeth, and his fingers turned white as he ground his hands into the boulder, he didn't move. The only action he allowed was to toss his head back and roar as hot jets of cum erupted to spray against my hand. His hips barely bucked, and I wasn't dislodged from a seat.

I continued to pump until he stilled my hand with his.

"You're going to kill me if you keep going," he gasped. "If you make me come again like that, I can't promise you won't end up on your pretty little ass in the grass."

My curiosity took over. "You'd be able to go again so soon?"

Was I an idiot for asking? Are guys usually able to repeat sex that quickly?

I wasn't inexperienced, but I wasn't that experienced either.

"We kept our gift of stamina." His wry smile was full of teeth. "No matter what promises were made, you know males wouldn't give that up."

I chuckled and tried to wiggle as little as possible getting off of him. He gripped my waist and helped me up.

"We can wash up quick, and then dry with that shirt. I'll need to wear pants back to the cabin. That shouldn't make anyone guess what we are up to." Guilt entered his expression. "Except Venus will know. And my brothers if they're back again. They'll know."

"How?"

"Our scents are mingled together."

I picked my way into the water, finding larger rocks to step on that weren't too slippery. "So shifters can go around and know who slept with who?"

He waded into the water like his feet were lined with lead. He turned his back, giving me privacy. "Basically. We grow up with the ability, so we don't think anything of it."

"Doesn't it cause issues?" I rinsed off.

He did the same and gestured for me to dry myself with the shirt first. "It can. Like I said, mating is sometimes an official arrangement, not one of the heart. We're not immune to jealousy."

I turned the shirt inside out in order to dry with the part of the fabric that I didn't orgasm on. "I guess some marriages are like that." I tossed him the shirt.

"Some mates are in an open relationship. Most mates are monogamous."

I should get dressed, but I was captivated while he dried off. Muscles bunching and flexing. Mesmerizing. He tossed his pants on. They were plaid flannel bottoms. I didn't know how I would explain those to Dad.

FOURTEEN

WE WERE SITTING around my dining room table thanks to a sudden rainstorm. Large drops buffeted against the window and thunder cracked through the night.

Penn finished telling the story about how he had the misfortune of falling asleep on the couch when he was twelve. Steel and I had given him our own versions of Sharpie tattoos. To retaliate, Penn had taken the markers and wrote *Deacon Was Here* or *Steel Was Here* on every women's bathroom stall he could get into without being noticed.

Venus's lips even curved up at the story. Since we'd returned, she hadn't spoken. I hadn't thanked her, but I needed to. Things had worked out better than I could've imagined. By the end of the weekend, maybe Ava would decide to keep her oath.

Penn leaned back in his chair, his gaze on Venus. I caught him looking at her several times throughout the evening. He was a Silver by clan and by name. He didn't have to try too hard to garner interest. It seemed he often avoided it, and his most common reason was studying. I didn't track his dating habits, but I'd also never seen him interested in anyone.

But maybe he was biding his time. Maybe he was waiting until he could shoot his shot with the daughter of the Jade ruling family.

"Are you heading back anytime soon, V?" Penn asked.

Venus took her time folding her white napkin into small squares. "I'd like to stay and see how everything plays out."

"Waiting to see if you still have a chance?"

"She's an official guest of mine," I interjected before Venus had a chance for a caustic reply or before Penn alluded to how envious Jades could be. I didn't know if he would, but I wasn't risking it.

Dorian was inspecting his plate like he regretted not turning in five minutes before Penn challenged Venus.

"You can't drive back in this weather," Ava added. My mate seemed to have developed a soft spot for Venus. Venus had terrified her, but like me, Ava sensed it had been for the best. It was what we had needed.

"It'd be no issue," Venus said, pinning Penn with a hard stare. "I've twenty years of experience driving."

Her comment was a subtle dig at their age difference. Steel choked back a cough and downed his lemonade to cover it up. I would almost feel bad for Penn, but he asked for it.

Penn wasn't going to just let it go. "Well, let me know if I can help. I can handle the curves in the dark."

Steel sputtered and gave up trying to stifle his laughter. Dorian couldn't even hold back a chuckle, and Ava put her hand over her mouth.

Dorian picked up his plate and took it to the sink. "I think it's time for this old man to get to bed."

"Are we going to Silver Lake tomorrow?" I asked.

Dorian scratched his neck. "I'm game if you are. But I know you've got a life. You don't need to be entertaining me all day."

"I never take a vacation. Work can get along without me for a weekend."

Venus took her plate to the sink. "I'm going to shamelessly use your Wi-Fi to watch some movies."

Penn grabbed his plate and Steel's. Since he never cleaned up after himself, I assumed I had Venus to thank for that too.

He set the plate next to hers on the counter. "Doesn't Jade Hills have fast internet yet? The infrastructure has been built in and around Silver Lake. It wouldn't be that big of a cost for the provider to build out to Jade Hills. But they'd have to sign on enough customers to make it worthwhile. But satellite service should—"

She ignored him and walked out of the room.

Steel blew out a breath. "I don't know what you're trying to do, Penn, but I don't think it's going to get anywhere with her."

Penn's expression turned to confusion. "What are you talking about?"

The three of us stared at Penn. Even Ava didn't believe him, and she had only known him for a few days. Steel and I were old enough to have rocked him to sleep and changed his diapers. We knew when he was lying, but he was completely oblivious to Steel's comment.

"Nothing," Steel muttered. "Why don't we see what slasher flick she's going to pick?"

Ava looked between them. "Venus likes horror movies?"

Steel smirked. "It's just a guess. She seems like a female who appreciates a good bloodbath."

Ava got up to load the dishwasher. I helped and wiped down the table. This was the domestic bliss I'd been holding out for.

Light flashed outside the window. "I love the sound of the rain, but storms like this make me nervous."

"Want to watch a movie with the others?" I wanted her to myself. All we would do was talk, and that would be enough. She wouldn't be comfortable doing anything more with everyone in the house.

"No. I'm not really in the mood to watch a movie right now." She glanced at the place where everyone had disappeared downstairs to watch a movie. She edged closer to me. "What do you look like when you shift?"

Mild shock rang through my veins. I was pleased she wanted to know but surprised that she was comfortable enough to ask. "Not much different from Venus, I imagine. Except I'd be a little bigger and have a silver sheen instead of green."

"So you all have different colors. What about when you mate between clans?"

"We're the ruling family, so our look matches our last name. Others just have a more dragony look."

She bit her lower lip like she was trying not to smile. "Dragony?"

"Like the stories I'm sure you heard as a little girl."

"The stories I heard as a little girl are more about big-bellied dragons that slept on their jewels all day. You mean more like *Game of Thrones*?"

I laughed. "Yes, less bellied and more *Game of Thrones*." I waited for more questions.

She remained quiet.

"You want to ask me something?"

She twined her fingers together and shifted her weight to her other foot. "Can I see it sometime?"

Hope surged inside me. After what we did together this afternoon, I was hopeful. But if she was intrigued enough to see my dragon? Then, as long as she didn't run away scared, Ava was mine.

"The rain is lightening up. Why don't we give it a little while, then I'll show you tonight?"

～

AVA

I COULDN'T BELIEVE I was doing this. The worst of the storm had passed. To the east, the sky was a heavy black with bolts of lightning highlighting banks of clouds. We shouldn't be outside, but nothing was going to drag me back in.

The smell of rain-soaked earth surrounded me. Deacon didn't lead me far into the trees, just enough to keep from getting seen by Dad. My dad's window faced a different direction, but Deacon didn't want to take the chance.

I pushed my hair behind my ears. At some point while Deacon was removing his clothing, my mouth started hanging open. I snapped my lips shut.

Deacon's eyes were as dark as the storm clouds. Nerves fluttered through my belly. Anticipation, not fear.

"Ready?" he asked.

I nodded but twisted my hands together in front of me. I had seen one dragon already, I could do it again.

A dragon.

The man I was falling hard for. A dragon.

This would be the moment. It would have to be. Everything he had told me and everything I had seen—I would need to make my decision. Do I move forward with this relationship, or cut it completely?

The change started. The same hologram effect I saw on Venus overlaid his face. His cheekbones sharpened and a silver sheen covered his hair and his skin. Then he grew impossibly large. I staggered backward a few steps but stopped myself.

My heart hammered, and I clasped my hands against my chest. His snout grew longer and his wings formed. There was no cracking of bones; it was a natural transition.

In less than thirty seconds, a bigger dragon than Venus stood in front of me.

Warm air whooshed out of his nostrils. A nervous giggle left me.

I reached a hand out, then snapped it back. His mighty head bobbed up and down. Eyes that were much larger than Deacon's, but still his, blinked. He dipped his head.

He was waiting for me to touch him. I took a tentative step forward. Was it my imagination, or did the air get warmer?

Drops of rain fell off the leaves at random intervals

around me. Where they landed on him, tiny tendrils of steam rose.

I stepped closer until I was within arm's reach. I touched my fingers to his snout. Smooth and hot, but not hot enough to burn. Pleasingly hot, as if hugging him would be like stepping into a sauna.

I ran my hand up his snout to between his eyes like I was petting the biggest horse I'd ever seen.

In the dark, his silver was subdued, but still more brilliant than Venus's green hue. "You're magnificent."

He didn't move, but an almost embarrassed huff came out of him.

All my hesitation fled. I ran my hands down his neck. The scales were harder than his face. That made sense. He remained still while I ran my hands along his back until I reached a wing. His smoldering pine scent was stronger than ever. I could bury my face against him and inhale for hours.

"Fascinating." His wing material was thin but tough. That didn't stop the strength that resonated from the structure. The wings were built to carry them through the sky. What was that like? To fly?

A beat of envy passed through me. What an ability to have. He could just fly to town to grab a carton of milk instead of driving.

No. Flying was too risky for them. Sadness fell from that thought like the collected raindrops rolled off the leaves.

They had sacrificed to keep from being wiped out. They had wanted what we had. And they had sacrificed for it.

I had never felt safer. Deacon was warm. I wasn't scared. I liked the dragon, but I wanted my guy back. All my nervous energy from before had nowhere to go. It needed an outlet. I needed to expend it, and all my thoughts were honed on Deacon.

"I really want you right now," I murmured.

His mighty head jerked around, and I looked straight into those big silver eyes.

He slowly held out his front limbs. Arms? With the claw—no, wait. A talon. He used a talon to gently lift my arms as he ducked his head. "You want me to put my arms around you?"

He nodded, using as little movement as possible to keep from knocking me down.

I did as he asked. I clung to him, and he wrapped his limbs around me. My feet lifted off the ground as he reared back. I instinctively smothered a scream. He couldn't be caught doing this. I would feel responsible if he got busted.

He gave me an extra squeeze as if to tell me to hold on. When I tightened my arms, he launched us into the air through the tree canopy.

My startled cry turned into a gasp. We were flying.

The trip only took seconds before we landed in the driveway behind all the vehicles. He had parked his pickup in the garage. Beside his vehicle was Dad's pickup. Then Venus's car and the pickup his brothers drove here.

Deacon gently took my arms from around his neck. And stood back.

The transition back to human man was faster than when he flowed into a dragon.

I didn't know what to say. The exhilaration of flight. The fascination of the other side of him.

"My pickup," was all he said.

I rushed to the rear passenger door and clambered in.

He crowded in behind me. For the second time that day, he removed my clothes. He tossed my garments into the front seat.

He tried to stretch out over me, but his head hit the roof. I tried to move a leg to make room for him and I kneed him in the gut. "Sorry."

"No problem."

He wedged himself between my legs. Our centers were off. His erection was pressing into my thigh. I adjusted my leg to the top of the seat. It helped, but not enough. He was too tall.

"Hold on." He maneuvered us until he was sitting in the middle of the back seat, and I was straddling him. I had to hunch over to rise up high enough to position him at my entrance. The broad head of his cock pushed inside. My thighs were quivering, trying to control the entry. His hot hands were around my ass. He was patient. He let me be in control. The hard planes of his face showed how rigidly still he was holding himself.

"I'm sorry." My body refused to open for him. I rocked up and back down, taking him in another inch.

"If it's not good for you, it's not good for me."

I pressed my hands against his shoulders and took more of him inside me. "It's good. I'm just—you're big and—"

He stuffed his hands through my hair and dragged my mouth down to his.

I relaxed under his incinerating touch. I sank farther down his length, continuing to take more of him until we were fully connected. He was everywhere inside me. With his size and the heat coming off of him, I didn't know where he stopped and I began.

I enjoyed being filled with him, but my body was

demanding more. Flexing my thighs, I rose and relaxed back down. A moan left me.

"Ride me, Ava," he said against my mouth.

I did just that. I rode him as fast and as slow as I wanted. He focused on my breasts bouncing in front of his face. Then I slowed down because I was ready to explode and I wanted to be with him longer. I didn't want to go back into the house and sleep by myself when I knew how nice it was to be with him.

It wasn't long before I couldn't back away from the peak anymore. My lower belly clenched and my inner muscles clamped around him.

I threw my head back and called out his name as I came. I had just crashed into my peak when heat bloomed inside me. He released, gritting out my name. It only amplified my ecstasy. I couldn't describe it. Sex had never been like this before. I bucked against him. He slid his hands around me and held me as we both finished.

I sagged against him and put my head on his shoulder. "What was that?" I got out between heavy breaths.

"What was what—oh. When we come, it's like an enhancement."

"I'll say," I mumbled. That was more potent than any sex toy. I raised my head with a gasp. "We didn't use any protection."

He kneaded my ass. "You're on birth control, correct?"

"Yes, but—"

"Then it's fine."

Babies weren't the only thing I was worried about. I wanted to have a family, but not now, not until I had no reservations about the person I was with. I had to decide whether I wanted to mate the father first. But babies weren't the only thing I was worried about. "Chance cheated on me a lot. I lost my job the day after we broke up and I went right home to Devils Lake, and Dad took me camping. I haven't had a chance to go into the clinic."

"It's all right." He continued to massage my flesh. He was still hard inside of me, and I couldn't bring myself to move off of him. "We don't get STDs."

"You don't?" I'd love not to have that worry. I went most of my life without the worry. Then Chance confessed to his many affairs.

"No. You'll still want to get tested, and I still want to smash your ex's face in. But if you're concerned about getting anything from me, or me getting anything from you, you can let it go."

"Oh." I'd had the biggest release in my life, then a giant adrenaline surge when I realized we hadn't used protection. I was back to being edgy. He skimmed his hands up my sides to cup my breasts. "You're ready again? I don't think I can be."

"Trust me, you are."

And I let him prove he was right.

FIFTEEN

D eacon

I woke up in the morning in my bed, alone. I had taken Ava three times in the back of my pickup last night. Then I had carried her into the house and tucked her in. I didn't care who else was awake, as long as her dad was sleeping. She was shy about what we did.

Today, I was taking Ava and her dad to Silver Lake again. My brothers would likely tag along. Until Ava said she would fulfill her oath, they wouldn't be far away. They knew I wouldn't mate anyone else. Not after being with Ava.

And Venus was still here. So that explained why Penn was around.

My birthday was in less than a week. The countdown was on. I could just as well have giant neon numbers above my head, ticking away the minutes in seconds until I turned thirty-five.

The council wouldn't give me any leeway. And I wouldn't let them. It'd be devastating, and it would be worse for my brothers. But as long as the big imaginary clock over my head was lit up, I still had time.

I had to believe there was a reason Ava was in the middle of that lake with her dad. There was a reason she had come back home, and her dad had suggested a camping trip. There was a reason I heard her shout that day. I couldn't believe anything different. We didn't have fated mates, but some things were just meant to be.

I rolled out of bed and jumped into the shower. Ava's almond cherry smell was all over my skin and I hated to wash it away. Sleeping with her scent around me was the next best thing to having her next to me. After I cleaned up, I went into the hallway. Ava's door was still closed. I had wanted to tuck her into my side and pull the covers over both of us so badly. If we had the house to ourselves, that might've happened. But Ava wanted to appear like a stable woman who was in charge of her life in front of her dad. I respected that.

I went out to the kitchen. It was empty, but the lingering scent of Dorian's shampoo told me he had just left. I liked that he didn't wear strong cologne. Shifters had a hard time with perfumes.

Steel and Penn came up the stairs.

Steel cocked a brow at me. "Have an exciting night?"

I scowled at him. "Don't you dare say anything and embarrass her."

Steel glanced down the hall. "I don't see her, so start talking. Did you claim her?"

"I haven't talked to her about that part yet."

Penn crossed to the cupboard and pulled out a glass. "Why didn't you take the chance when you had it?"

I bristled at his question. His tone was more curious than confused. It should be obvious I wouldn't betray her trust. It didn't matter if she thought a bite on her neck was foreplay or some sort of kink. I wouldn't do that to my mate until I talked with her. When my teeth touched her neck, she would be expecting it.

"We haven't gotten to that part yet. But I'm optimistic."

Steel snorted. "You'd better be more than optimistic."

"I won't trick her."

Steel leaned against the counter. "Then don't. Tell her the truth. Tell her that if she breaks her word, she's going to die."

"Shut the hell up."

We all heard Ava's bedroom door open. I shot Steel a hard glare and willed him to keep his mouth shut.

Ava shuffled across the hallway to the bathroom. When the bathroom door clicked shut, I hissed, "I am not pressuring her. Do you understand? If you tell her what breaking her oath means, I guarantee you will ruin this for us."

Steel clenched his jaw. "You're the boss. It's your life." He walked out of the kitchen, but in the living room he threw over his shoulder, "But remember that if your plan doesn't work, it affects more than just you and her."

He stomped to the front door. The door squeaked when he ripped it open. "Who the hell are you?"

I exchanged a confused look with Penn and rushed to the front door. A curvy brunette with wide brown eyes blinked at Steel. "Are you Deacon?"

I stopped behind Steel. "That's me. Who are you?"

The woman didn't take her eyes off Steel. "Where's Ava?" Her knuckles turned white as she clutched her phone in her hand. I could see enough of the screen to see she had emergency services pulled up. All she needed to do was hit the button to call them.

"You know Ava?" I asked.

She finally ripped her gaze off Steel to look at me, then she slid her distrusting gaze to Penn. "Where's Ava?"

Her other arm was curled around her back. The pungent smell of distrust wafted off of her. My brothers had to smell the same thing but refused to move. Penn inched back as if he sensed the woman's hostility rising higher.

"She just woke up. She's in the bathroom." I tried to muscle Steel out of the way, but he wasn't moving. I didn't want to elbow wrestle him in front of a woman who seemed ready to both call the police and attack us.

"Sure she is," she said sarcastically and craned her neck to look past us, but she was too short. "Ava! Ava, honey? Are you okay?"

"Do you think we've kidnapped her?" Steel snarled.

Tremors ran down the woman's body and she tensed like she was going to back up a step. Determination funneled into her expression. "Why isn't she answering?"

She didn't have time to hit the emergency call button. Steel snapped the phone out of her hands. The woman twisted her arm out from behind her back, a canister in her palm. But Steel caught her wrist and lifted it from her grip. The woman opened her mouth as she sucked in a breath. She was going to scream. No one would hear her, but I didn't want Dorian or Ava to get concerned. This was escalating too far too fast.

"Avril?" Ava's voice came from behind us.

The visitor snapped her mouth shut, and I twisted around. "Is she a friend of yours?"

Ava pushed between me and Steel. "She's my best friend."

Avril threw her arms around Ava. "Oh my god, are you okay?"

"She thought we kidnapped you." Steel sounded offended. He crossed his arms and glared at Avril. "Were you driving all night worried about Ava while she was having s—"

"Steel, shut up," I snapped. My mate didn't need to feel like crap for spending an amazing night with me.

He wasn't spared annoyance from Ava or Avril.

Venus appeared behind Avril. "Is there some weird force field around this house that attracts women?"

Ava let out a giggle but kept an arm around Avril's shoulders. "I think it's called the Silver brothers."

Avril gave Steel a pointed look. "Maybe their looks, but not their personality."

Venus laughed, her head tipped back. "This one's funny. Can we keep her?"

Alarm shot into Avril's eyes. Ava patted her on the shoulder. "She's joking. We were just heading to the lake. Want to come?"

Avril's nose wrinkled. I took in her shimmery tank top with the spaghetti straps and the pink shorts covered in gemstones. Her sandals had almost as much bling as her shorts. Avril wasn't an outdoor girl, or she wasn't planning to be an outdoor girl today. Had she come to check on Ava armed with nothing but pepper spray and her phone?

I appreciated her dedication as a friend. And I could capitalize on this moment. Ava had her dad with her, and now her best friend. If she saw her life integrating with mine, maybe she would be open to that claiming talk Steel asked about.

"Ava, if you'd like to stay with Avril, the guys and I can go to the lake. Venus too."

Venus rolled her eyes. "I might not want to go home, but hanging out with you guys with hooks in the water all day isn't what I want to do either."

"You can stay with me and Avril," Ava offered.

Venus scrutinized Ava as if she was trying to determine whether Ava was lying. Dragons could sense powerful emotions. Some of them even had their own smell. But Ava wasn't lying. Her invite was genuine. Honesty shone from her guileless blue-green eyes.

Venus's shoulders relaxed. She must've realized the same thing. "I guess. It sounds better than slimy rocks and slimier fish."

I'd miss spending time with Ava at the lake, but I liked having her in my house. Now that she had friends here, she was one step closer to being mine. She didn't need to know that her life depended on it.

∼

Ava

"Are you sure you're okay?" Avril whispered.

We were in the kitchen getting drinks. Venus was on the patio. The day started out gorgeous. Everything was drying after last night's rain. The bright sun streaming through the windows chased away any doubts about what happened last night. I couldn't forget. I couldn't believe I'd even slept, but he'd exhausted me.

Deacon had a lot of stamina.

"Ava?"

I startled. I was staring at the glass in my hand and not moving. No wonder Avril was worried. "I'm fine."

"We can leave right now." She was still whispering. Probably a good thing. Venus was outside, but she might still be able to hear. "Does she need to be rescued too?"

I giggled and went to the fridge. I took out the lemonade. "She can rescue herself. Trust me." I poured the glass and slid it over. "Did you have any breakfast?"

"I was so terrified." She shook her head. "I felt like you weren't telling me everything, and I just kept getting more worried."

She was pale. I should be the worried one. Avril must've left the city not long after I called her. I pushed the glass into her hands. "Drink. I'll make you some toast." I busied myself with breakfast while she leaned against the counter. "I'm sorry you felt like I was being dishonest. There are things about Deacon and his family I can't talk about." I shrugged. "They're not my secrets to tell. But I'm being honest with you about how I am. I can leave at any time, I just haven't tried."

"You believe him? And you really like him?"

I nodded and stared into the slots of the toaster. The bright-orange elements inside made me think of fire. And fire made me think of Deacon. All my thoughts circled back to him. "I really like him. It's just so soon. And he can't leave here. He's the mayor."

"You said after Chance you wouldn't change your life for a guy."

"I know. This is... different," I finished weakly.

Avril put her empty glass by the sink. She put a hand lightly on my shoulder. "After seeing what he looks like, I can understand. I don't want superficial reasons to be driving your decision."

"He's not Chance."

"I can see that."

The sliding door opened and Venus stepped through. She looked between me and Avril and how close we were standing. Her mouth tightened, and she started across the kitchen. Did she think we were avoiding her?

"Do you want some toast?"

Startled, Venus glanced over her shoulder. "I don't want to be a bother."

There was something in her tone that made me think she was talking about more than toast. Was she avoiding going back to her hometown because she felt like an imposition?

I didn't know enough about dragon shifters, but her people were trying to marry her off. If she had married—mated—Deacon, she would've moved to Silver Lake. Didn't she feel welcome at Jade Hills?

"We'd like to have your company. I'm starving, and Avril's been so worried about me." The toaster popped behind me, but I ignored it. "We grew up together. She moved to Minneapolis for college. When I went to visit her, I met a guy. Chance refused to move. So after school, I moved away from my parents, which I didn't really want to do. I moved in with Chance and found a job that wasn't really a good fit. Then Chance cheated on me and I got laid off."

Understanding lit Venus's green eyes. "History's repeating itself?"

"I was telling her that Deacon's nothing like Chance."

"He'll never cheat. He's one of the good ones like that." She lifted her chin toward the toaster. "I'm gonna burn right through carbs. I need to make eggs or something to go with it. Want some?"

Avril waved her hand between us. "I'm really confused. Aren't you Deacon's fiancée?"

Venus shook her head. "Deacon and I didn't make any promises to each other or anyone else about mate—marrying."

"So it really was an arranged marriage deal? I don't get it," Avril said.

"Pretend there's low-key royalty in Silver Lake and in my hometown, Jade Hills. And those two towns have a silly rivalry. I'm a princess, and Deacon's a king. The king needs a queen and the rivalry's causing problems. So our families thought we would be perfect together. Newsflash, we aren't."

"Why don't the towns settle it with football games like most small towns?" Avril asked.

"My family hasn't played fair in a single sport in history."

"Makes sense, I guess." Avril glanced at me before asking, "Do you think Deacon and Ava are perfect together?"

I wasn't sure I wanted to hear Venus's thoughts. "I don't—"

"They are perfect. You can see it in the way they look at each other when they think no one else is watching." Venus leaned forward and dropped her voice to a stage whisper.

"But I'm always watching." She straightened. In her normal voice, she said, "And I'm sure after all the sex they had last night, they realized how good they are together."

Avril gasped and rounded on me. Her eyes were wide. "What?"

Heat flushed my cheeks. Embarrassment made me want to melt into a puddle and run underneath the counters. Did everyone else in the house know what Deacon and I were up to last night? Did my dad know? How mortifying. "Things are moving kind of fast."

"Well, they kinda have to." Venus went to the fridge and dug out the eggs. Before I could ask her what she meant, she started gathering more ingredients. "I can make the best omelet you've ever had. Tell me what you want on it." She backed up and used her knee to shut the fridge door. "But don't tell the guys. I don't mind making a few omelets, but I'd have to make ten for them, and that's just a lot of work."

Avril asked what was on my mind. "Why do things have to move fast? It's Ava who's got to move and find a new job."

Venus stared at me for a moment. Her expression shuttered. I couldn't tell what she was thinking. "The agreement is that Deacon gets married by the time he's thirty-five."

"Okay..." Avril said. "And when does he turn thirty-five?"

Venus paused as if she didn't know how to answer. Then she blinked as if she realized something. "Ava, do you know when Deacon's birthday is?"

I shook my head. "When?"

She licked her lips as if she was figuring out how to

answer. Didn't she know? She had to know. Weren't their birthdays close together?

But all she said was, "You should ask him." With a bright smile that I didn't have to be a shifter to know was fake, she said, "Who likes a lot of cheese on their omelet?"

CHAPTER
SIXTEEN

THE IMPROMPTU GIRLS' day with Venus was fun. I didn't think Deacon expected to have a house full of guests when he invited me and my dad over, but I was enjoying myself. Growing up, it was me and my parents. I didn't get wild afternoons with a ton of cousins. I didn't have siblings to play with on camping trips. The overnights at Avril's house had been all I got.

There was never a dull moment at Deacon's. Right now, it was just me, Avril, and Venus. Deacon was still at the lake with Dad and his brothers. I liked seeing how he acted around them, and vice versa. When I had been alone with Chance, he acted differently than when he was around others. Subtly at first, and then a few snide comments were snuck in here and there. Toward the end, I had thought he was surly because of the stress of finding a job in his field. But the longer I was around Deacon, I realized it was me. Chance wanted to feel important, and he used me to achieve it.

Deacon wasn't like that. Or was I painting too pretty of a picture around Deacon? The reality was still that I didn't know him very well. We'd only known each other a week. When he met me, he wouldn't save Dad unless I swore myself to him. That was a red flag. A big old waving red flag.

Was I so willing to forget that?

Why wouldn't Venus tell me when his birthday was? It was just a birthday. I'd have to ask him, but for now, I was going to enjoy friend time.

Avril was sitting on the porch swing and letting it sway, her face tipped up to the sun. Venus was facing the same direction as Avril as she sat on the brick wall that also functioned as seating around the perimeter of the patio. I had spread a blanket over the grass and stretched out on it.

Puffy white clouds floated through the sky. The temperature would drop a couple of degrees when one temporarily blocked out the sun, but it was a nice reprieve from the heat. It was a beautiful day.

"What is Silver Lake like?" Avril asked.

"It's really beautiful," I answered. "Clear blue water and a ton of fish."

"No, the town."

I squinted at her. "I don't know. I haven't been there."

Avril gave me another look like she'd been giving me since she arrived. The type of expression that clearly asked how little I'd been thinking with my brain since I had arrived and how much I was letting my sex drive and my hurt pride run the show. "You're thinking of moving here and you haven't even been to town?"

I exchanged a look with Venus. Deacon couldn't be seen in town with me when everyone knew the arrangement that involved him and Venus. I shouldn't go to town with her either.

"It's a small town," Venus answered. "You know how those are. I'm sure Deacon wanted to win Ava over before the town exploded with ripe gossip."

The excuse was believable enough, and Avril nodded. "Devils Lake is bigger than Silver Lake, but is small enough to have the gossip. I get that."

Avril understood it better than me. There was a reason she moved so far away into a population high enough that she wouldn't run into anyone she knew at the grocery store. Blissful anonymity, she had called it.

"I'm not from here," Venus said. "If I show up in town with you two, everyone will just assume you're here for me. And they'll assume I'm here for Deacon."

She rose and straightened her shorts. I envied her long, toned legs, but I'd have to add another six inches to my height to compete with her.

Avril stopped the swing. "Are we going?"

I couldn't think of a reason why not. People would know who Venus was. Those who didn't would at least know what she was. And they would think Avril and I were with her. They might even think we were her bridesmaids.

Did shifter matings have bridesmaids?

As much as I liked it here, it would be nice to see what Silver Lake was like. It was the size of a typical small town in this area. A few hundred to a thousand people. But each town had its own charm, and if I was seriously thinking of moving here, which I couldn't believe, then I should visit it once before I left.

I had the urge to call Deacon and ask for permission. That was exactly the type of relationship I was avoiding. I stood, taking the blanket with me, and shook it out. "Do you mind driving? I want to leave the truck here for Dad, in case he needs anything."

"It wouldn't be the Venus Jade experience if it wasn't for my little red car."

~

DEACON

WE CAUGHT our limit and were packing up to head home.

Dorian slid the tackle box into the bed of the pickup. "Either you guys are good luck, or I only learned how to fish this week."

I chuckled and shut my tailgate. "That's why Silver Lake's our secret. It's a small town, and we like to fish. Can't have all the out-of-towners siphoning our supply."

Dorian shook his head, his grin still in place. "I tell you what... I just can't believe it." Each fish he caught was like his first. No wonder the man had stuck with the sport for decades. He loved it.

The crunch of tires in the distance caught my attention. Both of my brothers looked at the entrance to the parking area by the lake. Someone was coming. I hadn't lied to Dorian. The lake was decent sized, and many people didn't fish here since it was my property. So whoever was heading this way was someone we would know.

Seconds later, a small gray sedan coasted into the parking lot.

I wanted to groan when I saw it was Bronson. He'd better be here to fish. I had sent the council a report that the feral mountain lion shifter had been put down. The only other topic I'd have to discuss with Bronson was Venus and my impending birthday.

He parked next to my pickup. He didn't take his time getting out of his car. His gaze brushed over my brothers and settled on Dorian.

"Going to catch some dinner?" I asked him. I strode toward him to keep the conversation away from Dorian. Since Bronson wore a pale-pink shirt tucked neatly into navy blue trousers, I didn't get the impression he was here for outdoor recreation.

Steel waved at Bronson. Then he turned his attention to Dorian. "Go ahead and take the front seat. Penn and I will ride in the back." It was as subtle an order as any to get into the pickup. I tossed Steel my keys to start it and get the AC going. I didn't know how long Bronson would talk, or what he had to say, but no reason for my guests to bake while waiting.

"You know I'm not here to fish, Deacon." Bronson's tone was a mixture of urgent, irritated, and alarmed.

"I gathered that."

"Venus is in town."

I nodded. Had she gotten along with Ava and Avril? Or did she run to town for supplies? I hadn't been prepared for so much company. I probably needed groceries.

"She wasn't alone." Bronson's gaze darted to my pickup. He dropped his volume. "She had two humans with her."

My brows shot up. Venus took the other two into town with her?

Shit. It was my fault. I couldn't hold Ava prisoner. It wasn't her problem that we met so close to my birthday. But I had hoped to keep this from the council until I had completely won her over.

Last night had to mean something. Ava was too self-conscious, too insecure, to be intimate with someone she didn't trust. She was so close to being mine—but she wasn't yet.

Time was short, but I was also the leader. The council trusted me and I hadn't been honest with them. "Venus and I don't want to mate each other."

Bronson's brows drew together. "You two made an oath."

The council loved making it sound that way. It hadn't been a big enough deal to correct them over the years. "Each of our councils told us what they had decided, and we didn't argue. We were kids. When we were older, I called her to talk about it. She said she didn't have plans to defy it if I didn't. At the time, I didn't have a reason to, so we didn't fight it."

Bronson propped his hand on the top of his car and slammed the other one on his hip. "And you're saying you have reason to now? Does it have to do with one of the two humans she's with?" His gaze traveled to my pickup. "Or the human you have with you?"

"Yes."

"Your clan is counting on you. Jade's clan is counting on Venus. If you and Venus mate, it would do a lot to diminish the animosity between us. We don't know enough about Lachlan to trust he's not like his parents."

Venus's brother didn't care about anyone's authority

except his, but he seemed to care about his people. Since he'd taken over, I hadn't had to deal with feral shifters in or around Jade Hills. When I heard about some Jade shifter fucking with Silver Lake property, I had approached him. All he'd said was that he'd dealt with it and it wasn't my business. Since the problems hadn't recurred, I'd chosen to believe him and leave my ego out of the confrontation.

Perhaps ignoring his attitude hadn't dealt with the animosity between our people, but I had to believe it'd get there. Lachlan wouldn't change things overnight, and neither would I. Likewise, suddenly being Venus's mate wouldn't make people think different in a day or two.

Lachlan, Venus, and I had a lot of pressure as it was. I didn't need people insisting we behave a certain way for their own personal reasons. "Look, Bronson, I know you and Michael are waiting to mate after me and Venus, but I don't appreciate my future getting tampered with because you're too afraid to incur Jade clan's wrath."

Bronson clenched his jaw, but chagrin flashed in his eyes. "The council's decision had nothing to do with our personal lives, and my insistence that you abide by the contract doesn't either. Yes, our relationship highlights some problems between us. His family dislikes me because I'm Silver. His car was keyed when he went to grab milk the other day. But we're handling it. We've been handling it for five years."

Surprise pushed out my annoyance. I didn't know Bronson and Michael had been dating for that long. Bronson's first mate had passed away from a massive heart attack. He had stayed single for a long time. Perhaps that was why he had kept his time with Michael quiet. "I know Venus isn't her brother, but I get along with her. I can be professional with Lachlan, and that's more than our parents could do. Isn't that a start?"

"Not when the entirety of Jade clan will think you shunned her. Are you into one of those other girls? Does it matter, or are you desperate not to mate Venus?"

I couldn't keep my secret any longer. Bronson would know I was lying otherwise. "I have a connection with one of them. I want her to be mine. But she's human, and it's taking her time to come around."

"And I'm guessing she doesn't know Venus is the equivalent of your fiancée?"

"She knows."

Bronson pushed off his car and crossed his arms. "Are you admitting that you told a human about us without being certain that she was going to mate with you?" He squeezed his eyes closed and shook his head. "Does she realize how badly you endangered her life?"

Being responsible for someone's death is an enormous incentive to keep from randomly telling humans about us. Once Bronson left, he would tell the council about Ava and her knowledge of our kind. They'd put a target on her back.

And they would expect me to be the one to carry out the punishment. Or perhaps they would think it was compassionate to pass the task onto my brothers. Neither option was going to happen. I could buy some extra time by telling the truth, as much as I hated exposing Ava. "She swore herself to me."

Bronson shook his head as if he was dislodging mud from his ears. "I'm sorry, what?"

"She swore an oath."

He stared at me as if I was a three-headed dragon.

"Then why aren't you mated? You have days—*days*—before you need to be taking vows of your own."

"And I'm using those days so she doesn't resent being rushed into a lifelong decision."

Bronson threw his hands in the air. "But that's exactly what you did! And what about the agreement between the clans? You're passing up their leader's sister for a human. It won't matter if your little human is Venus's new BFF. Maybe Lachlan won't care, but he's going to be pressured to make our clan pay."

"I'm not saying this isn't going to cause problems. But like you said, I have days. Let me figure this out."

"There's nothing to figure out. If your human is alive after you turn thirty-five, then she has to answer for breaking her oath, *and* we have a major problem with Jade."

"I have time, Bronson," I said in a harsh tone. My patience was draining at an alarming rate and I didn't need to be reminded of everything at stake.

"You really think you can pull this off?"

"I have to believe I can." If I could go back again, I would've saved Dorian and spent the rest of my life trying to forget Ava. The risk to her was too great.

"You'd better hope there's some solution that doesn't end up with one or both of you in the grave with two clans at war."

CHAPTER
SEVENTEEN

A^{va}

"I SUPPOSE WE SHOULD HEAD BACK." Venus had the top down on her convertible. She'd parked at the edge of the ice cream shop parking lot. Avril had bought us all sundaes.

Avril finished a mouthful of her butterscotch sundae. "I don't know if I'm ready. I don't think I've been stared at quite enough."

Venus giggled, holding the back of her hand against her lips so ice cream wouldn't drip out. "The whole town will be talking tonight. You two are going to be famous." She put her ice cream container in her cupholder and started the vehicle. "Which means we should probably get back. I'm sure someone's tattled to Deacon by now."

"But they're at the lake," I said, swirling my hot fudge and peanuts into a chunk of ice cream.

"It doesn't matter. I'm sure I'll get a call from my brother any second."

"What's your brother like?" I asked.

Venus pulled out of the parking lot. "He used to be sort of laid back. Now he's a grump."

"That's too bad," Avril said.

Venus lifted her shoulder as she draped her hand over the wheel.

"I don't have any siblings," I said. "But I would've liked some."

Venus glanced at me and focused back on the road.

I got the sense she wanted to say something. Or had I said something wrong? "I'm sorry. I didn't mean to diminish your troubles with your brother."

She shook her head. "It's not that. Guys from, you know, Silver Lake and Jade Hills?" She lifted her gaze to the rearview mirror, and I understood what she wasn't saying. Shifters. "They tend to go for only children, those without siblings."

Understanding dawned on me. Shifters naturally fell for an only child, making it less complicated about what they would tell family. "Oh."

"So if it wasn't for Ian..." Avril set her empty ice cream cup in the holder next to Venus's. "I might end up with someone from Silver Lake or Jade?"

Venus's gaze flickered, but she laughed. "You never know. Lachlan is mated, but I have a younger brother. He's kind of a dick though."

"I'll stick with Ian. One of these days, he'll actually propose when he's kneeling and not trying to go viral by tricking me." Her brown hair buffeted around her face as she stared at the passing scenery and hid her expression.

Venus met my gaze in the rearview mirror. She cocked

a brow. I lifted a shoulder as if to tell her I thought Avril would be better off without him too.

Avril looked at her reflection in the side mirror. "He thinks I should go blonde."

"Nope." Venus raked her gaze over Avril's hair. "Your shade of brunette is what I have several clients paying to get, and blonde doesn't complement your skin tone."

"You're a stylist?" Avril asked, and I realized I hadn't asked Venus much about her personal life.

"Yes, but I don't get to work on many young women. I have a few regulars. Anyway, if you came in asking to go blonde, I'd ask about your motivation. 'Because a guy wants it' is not a good enough reason to bleach your hair. Look at your natural highlights. Seriously, people pay a lot of money for those. They call us envies for a reason."

"What about mine?" I asked before Avril asked more about the envy thing. Besides, I always found my hair color dull, but I hadn't had spare money for a treatment and I didn't trust myself to DIY it. Venus seemed like a stylist who'd want to make her clients feel better about themselves, not push her own preferences on them.

"Your color is perfect for you, but you'd be the exception to my 'because a guy wants it.' I'm afraid of what Deacon would do to me if I suggested you change it—which I don't. Your color is shiny, healthy, and lovely. Deacon eyes your hair like it's a precious metal."

"But it's not silver," I joked.

Venus snorted a laugh, and Avril chuckled. I caught my friend eyeing her brown locks in the mirror, a new appreciative expression on her face. Venus might not know the impact she made, but Ian's suggestion must've bothered Avril. The guy had a way of making her feel like she wasn't enough.

The drive to Deacon's place took several minutes. When Venus drove through the trees surrounding his property, his pickup came into view. She parked in the same spot as before.

Deacon came around the side of the house. I waved and hopped out while Venus and Avril put the top of the Mercury back into place.

"Hey!" I called. "Did you have any luck?"

He smiled, but there was tension in his expression that wasn't there this morning. "Caught our limit. Your dad said we're spoiling him."

As I approached, I asked quietly, "What's wrong?"

"Take a walk with me?"

I nodded. It must be shifter business. I hollered to Avril, "Go on in. I'll be back."

Avril studied Deacon, but her hostility from the morning was gone. Distrust resonated in her expression, but she'd been here less than a day. That was progress.

Deacon slid his arm around my back and dropped a quick kiss on my lips. "I missed you."

I loved hearing those words. He made me feel important. I didn't realize how that had been missing from my last relationship. "I missed you too. Did everything go all right at the lake?" He stared ahead of us. The sunlight overhead lightened the blue of his eyes. They were no longer a stormy blue. More like an after-the-storm blue.

"Your trip to town didn't go unnoticed."

I dropped my head. Dammit. I didn't want a relationship where I had to stay in the cycle of seeking approval.

"That's not what's upsetting me." Deacon stroked my back as we walked. "It's my fault for not telling the council about the change in plans. But I want you to have as much time as possible to make your decision. I don't want to pressure you."

The first couple of days after we met, he had made the oath sound like a much bigger deal than it seemed to be. Now, he wanted to give me time. I hated feeling like I didn't deserve someone like Deacon. Extremely attractive. Considerate. And attentive.

But why didn't I? I had grown up witnessing every day how close my parents were. Their relationship was full of love, trust, and respect. I wasn't settling for anything less, and maybe that was what was keeping me in Silver Lake. Maybe Deacon was that guy.

"I appreciate it." We walked to the edge of the trees but stopped before the main gravel road that ran past his place. "Is that what's bothering you?"

"Yeah, it is. Bronson—a council member—just put a lot of pressure on me. He's afraid of how Venus's brother will react. I asked him to wait to tell anyone until your decision was finalized. You don't need the extra stress."

I had a sense he wasn't telling me everything, but I pushed the thought away. I had a fun day with friends. A day hanging out with my lifelong best friend and a brand-new friend that I would've considered out of my league. And all of that had followed the most intensely pleasurable night I had ever experienced.

"Thank you."

He faced me and hooked his hands around my back. "The only thing I want you worrying about is helping me figure out a new recipe to make with all the fish we caught. And to stay away from the house long enough that my brothers and your dad can finish cleaning what we caught."

I laughed and stuffed my hands into his hair. When

his mouth crashed into mine, I knew we wouldn't have an issue wasting time before we returned. And I would enjoy every minute.

Because I had already made my decision. But I would appease the part of me that was still raw from the way Chance treated me. I would wait a full twenty-four hours before I told Deacon my decision.

~

DEACON

AVA WAS LISTENING to her dad tell her the story of each catch. I was manning the grill. We had decided on putting together several foil packets of fish with different flavorings.

Avril and Venus chatted on the patio wall. Venus was leaning back with her long legs stretched out. I only knew because I had to see what Penn kept glancing at.

Steel edged closer to me. "You gonna tell me about Bronson yet?"

"It's just what you would think. As if he has to tell me the consequences. They're crystal fucking clear."

"And you haven't told Ava what's at stake?"

I scowled at him. He knew I hadn't. "I told Bronson the same thing I told you and Penn. I'm giving her the chance to make this decision naturally."

"You've got some pretty big balls, even for a Silver male."

I chuckled, but the humor wasn't there. I hated to be reminded what the council was within their right to do if Ava refused to mate me.

"And where the hell are you going to put everybody?" Steel grumbled.

I glanced at all my guests. It was a five-bedroom house, but Steel and Penn were switching out who slept on the floor in my office and who slept on the couch. "I'm sure Avril will room with Ava."

"You need to send her on her way."

I gave him an *are you crazy* look. "Why would I do that? I think Ava's relaxed more since she's gotten here."

Avril had brightened the shadows that still lingered in Ava. Being at my place with her dad wasn't enough. Ava missed her friend. And to everyone's surprise, she had made friends with Venus. Ava was thriving at my place, and I had Avril, in part, to thank.

"You have a house full of three humans, and the council knows about your shenanigans. You've already put Ava at risk. The other two are at risk by association."

The sun was hours from setting, but Steel's comment darkened my mood. "I'm handling it."

Penn crowded on the other side of the grill. "We're worried. We don't want to clean up a mess."

I glared at both of them. "I've been cleaning up all the messes. Just like Dad wanted. You two don't have to lift a finger. A free ride off the Silver name."

"Harsh," Penn said.

I expected Steel to tell me to piss off and storm away. I was being unfairly harsh. They had every reason to worry. But he leaned closer. "Don't equate your unwillingness to ask for help with our level of contribution. Penn and I make sure a lot of messes don't even reach you."

Steel was my younger brother by three years. He'd been a full-grown adult for a long time. But I didn't expect him to sound so commanding. I also didn't expect to believe him. What had been going on that I didn't know about?

Before I could inquire, Ava and Dorian rose from the porch swing. She aimed her sunny smile my way. And just like that, I didn't care about Silver Lake's dark secrets.

"Can we help with anything?"

"She could make most of this go away," Steel muttered loud enough for me to hear as he turned away. "I'll set the table."

Penn followed him. Ava frowned at their backs. When she met my gaze, I shrugged and hoped she attributed the tension to what happened with Bronson today. Technically, that would be accurate. Minus the part about her life being on the line.

CHAPTER

EIGHTEEN

VENUS WAS **exceptional** at both cornhole and bocce ball.

"Cheater," Penn called. He and Deacon were on the opposing team. And they were losing at the current game of cornhole.

Venus weighed the second sandbag in her hand. Her eyes were narrowed when she glanced at me. "Ava, how badly do you want to win?"

"I mean…" I wasn't a very competitive person. Avril probably should've been her partner.

Venus must have interpreted my answer as not being too tied to the outcome because she cocked her arm back and whipped the beanbag. It slammed into his shoulder.

"Oomph." Penn staggered back a couple of steps as Deacon barked out a laugh.

176

"Oh, sorry," Venus said in an innocently sweet voice. "My aim was a little off."

Penn juggled the bag from hand to hand. "I think that's a disqualification."

Deacon, still laughing, smacked him on the back. "I think she was aiming for your head."

"If you start spouting cornhole rules"—Venus used the same saccharine tone—"I'll make sure to aim at your head."

"Believe, no one's interested in the rules." Penn swung his arm to encompass our gaming area. "For one, our playing area is supposed to be level, you've stepped out of the pitcher's box at least five times, and we haven't marked a single foul line."

"And there he goes," Venus muttered. "Game over. I'm out."

Confusion sparked in Penn's expression as if he didn't realize his recitation of the rules we broke annoyed her.

I helped pick up the lawn game equipment. The sun was setting and the shadows of the trees stretched almost completely across the yard. We'd feasted on several variations of grilled fish, and then played games.

Avril had gone to bed a couple of hours ago. She had been exhausted from traveling so long. Dad turned in about an hour ago.

Venus lifted the wooden cornhole platforms as if they weighed no more than a shoebox. I was following her across the yard when a scream ripped through the night.

My heart jumped into my throat and I whirled around. Where did that come from?

Deacon was beside me in a second. "Go into the house, Ava."

"What was that?"

"Mountain lion."

"But it sounded like a scream."

He put his hands on my shoulders and herded me toward the patio. The smell of the citronella candles surrounded me as I got closer to the house.

"Mountain lion shifter. Go inside and make sure Avril and your dad stay there in case they wake up."

I had a million questions. Why would mountain lion shifters be screaming in the trees around Deacon's house? But he had just put down one of their kind. One that was supposedly feral. I was too new to shifter politics, but it was probably safe to assume that the feral had loved ones left behind who didn't agree with the killing.

In the house, I went to the kitchen window and peered outside. My breathing was ragged in my ears, but I tried to calm myself.

Was Avril awake?

There was no sound in the house. I couldn't see Deacon or his brothers or Venus in the backyard anymore. Another scream cut through the night, muffled because I was now inside. I crouched down as if that thing could see me through the windows. I didn't want to go into my room and wake Avril up if she had slept through the noise. Dad slept through thunderstorms whenever we were out camping. I doubted he would wake up. Creeping through the house, I kept the lights off until I got to Deacon's room. I snuck up to his bedroom window, which also faced the back of the house. With a shaking hand, I peeked through the blinds.

It was dark out. I couldn't tell if the rustle of leaves was from the wind or from a mighty dragon weaving between the branches.

A scream rose in pitch and cut off. What was happening?

Another scream wailed and ceased just as quickly as the previous one. I jerked my hand out of the blinds and jumped into the middle of Deacon's bed.

How many shifters were out there? It couldn't be more than four dragon shifters could handle. Could it?

If I stayed with Deacon, would this be my life?

Would we be having a family barbecue in the back-yard and then some pissed-off shifter with a grudge would try to hurt one of us?

I didn't want that to be the case. But it made an already complex decision so much more complicated.

I buried my head in my knees, wishing I could help, but I wasn't qualified to be outside of these walls. I kept listening for movement in the house. It was my job to intercept Avril and my dad if they woke up. That was the least I could do.

The floor creaked, and I jerked my head up. A large shadow took up the doorway. After a quick spike of fear, I calmed down. I couldn't see definition but I knew Deacon's shape.

"Is it over?" My voice shook more than I meant it to. I wanted to seem strong. Impossible, since he found me cowering in his bed.

He crossed to me, shutting the door behind him, and crawled into the bed, gathering me in his arms. He didn't have any clothes on. They were probably still in the woods, or maybe he dropped them on the floor.

"You're safe." He rubbed my back. "It was just some young shifters. Part of the feral shifter's old pack. The equivalent of dumb teenagers. They were just messing around, thought it would be funny."

"Did anybody get hurt?"

"No. They weren't expecting my brothers to be here, and definitely not Venus. They ran away so fast that I think they'll be stiff for the next month." A deep chuckle rumbled in his chest. "I'll have a talk with their elders, but it was nothing more than a prank."

Relief washed through me, but it wasn't as cleansing as I had hoped. What if the next time it wasn't just young kids being immature?

Gentle fingers lifted my chin. "It's okay, Ava. This hasn't happened before. Most shifters want to live in peace."

"But it could happen again?"

The harsh angles of his face were prominent in the dark. He nodded and said a soft, "Yes."

He could have tried to lie. I would've known, but he could've tried anyway. Instead, he told the truth. Instead of a reply, I pressed my lips to his.

DEACON

As soon as her mouth was on mine, my body reacted. The adrenaline surge from earlier was looking for an outlet. Chasing a bunch of overgrown kids off hadn't dented it.

The scent of her terror tinged the air. She'd been scared for herself, but she'd been terrified for me and the others. And she was smart enough to know that making a life with me meant that we could have a repeat of tonight.

I needed to reassure her, needed her to know that I

would do everything I could to keep her safe. The words didn't come, but I could show her.

I pressed her backward until she was stretched out on my covers. Dragging her shorts over her hips and down her legs, I didn't break our kiss. I had to part from her long enough to get her shirt over her head. Then the bra was gone, and she was naked underneath me.

She parted her legs wide enough to fit me between. I should go down on her. I should get her ready for me. But I didn't want to wait. I needed that connection, that confirmation that she was mine. I needed to show her.

I stroked my erection through her growing wetness. Back and forth as she rocked her hips against me. When I thought I could enter her without hurting her, I pushed inside.

This time, she knew what to expect. Her mind and body knew my size and knew that there was no more perfect fit than me.

I let out a quiet growl once I was seated fully inside of her. Her heat surrounded me and her inner walls clenched around my erection, milking me, encouraging me to move. So I did.

I kept my mouth on hers and swept my tongue inside. I wanted to taste her. The sweet flavor that was Ava. The woman who worried about me. The woman who had been here when I'd returned from one of the worst parts of my job. The woman I wanted to be my mate.

A needy moan left her. I swallowed what sound I could. My thrusts were coming faster and the pressure inside me coiled tighter. Since the first time I came inside of her, I knew this was what I wanted to do for the rest of my life. I knew that if she rejected me, there would be no one else. If she rejected me, I wouldn't take another. I would protect her.

She didn't know what that meant, but I did. And I was prepared for it.

Her knees drew up higher and her heels pressed into my ass. We were both going to come fast and hard together.

My orgasm erupted from my rock-hard balls, exploding at the same time as she arched underneath me.

Our climaxes matched in speed and intensity. Another sign of how this was meant to be.

Did she see it? Did she know? Had tonight ruined it?

Somehow, we had stayed quiet, as far as humans were concerned. I stroked her sides and ran my thumbs around the curve of her breasts. I lifted my head to stare into her eyes.

"I want to stay like this for just a little longer."

I couldn't bring myself to say more. I couldn't bring myself to tell her I was terrified she was going to leave me. I couldn't bring myself to tell her she might've been the one to make an oath, but I was going to be the one to lose everything if she broke it. Even if she rejected me, that would be my final gift to her.

She feathered her fingers down my face. "I'd like that. I'd like to stay with you in your bed tonight."

Relief raced like a tidal wave down my back, and I grinned. "I'd like that too."

In that moment, I wasn't worried. She wouldn't spend the night with me in bed and then walk away.

CHAPTER

NINETEEN

I woke up next to a wall of muscle. I had slept with him. All night.

What would Avril think? Her first night in a strange house and I had ditched her. Of course, she could never know about the mountain lion shifters harassing us. But I hadn't even checked on her.

I rolled toward the side of the bed that didn't have a big slumbering man. I planned to scoot quietly out and listen by the door to hear if anyone else was awake.

A hot hand landed on my bare hip. That was right. I was naked. I didn't even know where my clothes were. Probably on the floor.

"Where are you going?" Deacon asked in the sexiest morning rumble.

"I was going to sneak back to the other bedroom."

"It embarrasses you?"

Did I hurt his feelings? "No, but it seems rude to have just left Avril."

"She's still sleeping. No one's woken up yet. You think she would be upset with you?"

I doubted it. After a fun night of grilling and lawn games, she probably didn't think I was making a huge mistake. Avril wasn't shy about her opinions. I should've listened to her from the very beginning about Chance. "No, I don't think she would be upset."

"Good, because I have plans for what we can do until everyone wakes up."

I tensed. Having sex in the pickup's back seat was fine when my hair was brushed out and I had a touch of lip gloss on. Having sex last night was also fine—it had been dark.

But it was morning. Enough light streamed through the blinds to show Deacon just how my fine hair turned into a rat's nest by morning. And I went to sleep last night before I could brush my teeth.

After a full night of sleep, all I wanted was my toothbrush. "I just need to run to the bathroom—"

"You're already gorgeous, and I love the way my scent's clinging to you."

I looked over my shoulder at him. "I don't feel fine."

He was undeterred as he prowled toward me. I squeaked and tried to scramble out of bed. I was stopped by a pair of strong hands gripping my hips.

He angled my ass in the air and rose to his knees behind me. "If you give me a couple of seconds, I can chase all those worries away."

Whether it was his voice or being naked in bed with

him, or that my body now seemed to be primed for him at all times, it worked.

I arched my butt higher and stretched my hands out in front of me. "Promise?"

He answered "promise" as he shoved inside. I buried my face in the sheets to keep from crying out. Our first time last night had been fast and furious, but then he'd transitioned into a long round of lovemaking that had been like a marathon. This was a sprint, and it was exactly what I needed. I didn't worry about my hair; I didn't worry about my breath. All I had to concentrate on was the pleasure expanding inside of me and morphing into pure, unadulterated ecstasy.

We came together again. I didn't know how that happened. Was it a shifter thing? Or was it an us thing? But as I orgasmed, he was releasing inside me and the heat soldered us together.

As his bucking slowed and he planted his weight on a hand next to me while he stroked my back with his other hand, I said, "I want to stay with you. I want to be yours."

He went still. "Do you mean that?"

"Yes." I didn't give him a list of reasons why. The answer was simply yes.

"Ava, you don't know how fucking happy I am to hear that."

He pulled out of me and stretched out behind me. He curved a strong arm around my torso and buried his nose in my hair.

"I want to mate you as soon as possible, but first I'm going to take you one more time in the shower."

~

I squeezed Avril tight. "Drive safe and call when you get there."

"I'm going to message you at every stop and make sure you're okay."

She didn't bother to lower her voice. I couldn't see her face while we were hugging, but I wouldn't be surprised if she was trying to shoot Deacon a menacing look. She pulled back and brushed a lock of dark hair behind her ear.

"I wish I didn't have to work tonight."

"I know. I'm going to miss you." Avril didn't know I decided to stay with Deacon. I didn't know if she could be involved in the mating ceremony, but it wasn't like I could ask right in front of her. She didn't like leaving as it was. I didn't want her to feel left out, especially if she couldn't be involved.

"I'd wait for your dad to wake up, but I won't have enough time for more than two potty breaks as it is. Tell him bye for me?"

"Of course." We hugged again, keeping it brief.

Then Avril shouldered her bulky tote bag, gave Deacon a wave, and rushed out the door. I watched her drive away before I sank into a kitchen chair.

Deacon sat next to me.

"Can Dad be there for the ceremony?"

Deacon paused. From his expression, I could tell he didn't want to answer. Which meant I could figure out what he was going to tell me.

"Only shifters allowed in the ceremony?" I asked.

He gave me a sympathetic smile. "It would definitely seem weird to him. He might be comfortable with all this, but some of the verbiage in our ceremony would make him wonder if you were getting tricked into a cult."

The way Deacon had won Dad over, I doubted Dad would be too worried about a cult Deacon and his brothers were in.

"I can tell him I'm staying. He's supposed to go back to Devils Lake tomorrow anyway." Dismay took over my excitement. I couldn't have my dad or my best friend at the ceremony?

Deacon closed his hand over mine. "We can always have a wedding celebration, even a ceremony, with your loved ones. But the mating ceremony will need to be shifter only. If you'd like, it can just be you and I with the council member. Neither of us will have anyone there."

I frowned. A private ceremony with just us would be fine. I hadn't met the shifters on the council, but it didn't seem right that he wouldn't have anyone there. "No, you should have your brothers."

"We'll have a wedding ceremony wherever you want it. Devils Lake, or Minneapolis if Avril can get off work. It doesn't matter. As long as you're mine." The way his eyes warmed was like being next to his physical dragon.

"I feel like I should wear more than the shorts and the T-shirts I've been wearing since I've been here."

"All that matters is the vows, Ava. All that matters is that we're sworn together. I don't care about appearance, and I don't care about celebrations."

I cared a little, but when I got right down to it, I realized that was only because I thought others would care. Being with Deacon was all I wanted. I liked his brothers and how comfortable I felt around them. The small town of Silver Lake was charming. I didn't know yet what I would do for work, but I was confident I would find something here or in Wildrose, or even online. I was going to take my time and find something that called to me. Life insurance sales did not call to me.

Steel and Penn entered the kitchen. Steel eyed our connected hands and raised a brow toward his brother.

Penn let out a low whistle. "Congrats, man. I'm glad to hear everything worked out."

Deacon gave my hand a squeeze. "Now that they're up, I'm going to the office to call Bronson. He can come out and do the ceremony tomorrow after your dad leaves."

I smiled but dropped my gaze from the way the two brothers were looking at me with still solemn gazes. It seemed like they were happy for Deacon, but it also seemed like they wouldn't relax until we said I do, or whatever it was dragon shifters said.

I was basically getting married. How much had my life changed since last week? But I couldn't escape the sense that this felt right. I felt like I was making the right decision.

Deacon released my hand. He kissed the top of my head as he rose, then he went downstairs.

He greeted Dad on the way down. Dad entered the kitchen and took the chair that Deacon was in. "Our time here has almost come to an end. My boss called and asked if I could come back a couple days early. They had a hailstorm and they're swamped with claims."

I wouldn't have wanted to leave early. So this was it. "I wanted to talk to you about that, Dad."

He gave me a knowing smile. "You want to stay?"

It was easier to talk to him about this than Deacon's brothers. Dad was oblivious to the mating ceremony and all that it meant. That must be why there was still an air of anxiety circling Steel and Penn. "I'd like to stay a little longer. Deacon will take a few days off, and we'll come grab my things."

Dad's eyes misted over. His gaze swept over where the brothers were making breakfast at the counter. "I'll have my phone on me. You need anything—*anything*—call me. I'll be here as soon as humanly possible."

I managed not to snort when he used the phrase *humanly possible*. I leaned forward and wrapped my arms around him. "Thank you. We're still figuring everything out, but I want to stay here. Really."

He patted my back. "I'm happy for you." He dropped his voice to a whisper. "But you call if you need anything."

I was nodding again when Deacon appeared at the top of the stairs. His expression was pensive, but he didn't immediately say anything, so I didn't ask.

Dad stood. "I reckon I've been in your hair long enough. I'm going to finish packing, and I'll grab some breakfast on the road."

Deacon's expression immediately turned pleasant. "Are you leaving early?"

"Eh, work called. I reckon I'll save the vacation to come back out and check on Ava."

"You're welcome anytime. Consider the room you've been in yours. You sure you don't want to stay for some breakfast?"

Dad chuckled and shook his head as he started down the stairs. "You have a mighty big grocery trip ahead of you after a houseful of guests for almost a week. No, I'll be fine. I'm full up to my eyeballs with fish. I can wait before I grab a bite."

When Dad was gone, Deacon came all the way into the kitchen, but he didn't sit down. He exchanged looks with his brothers before his gaze settled on me. "Bronson said we need to go to city hall. He'll perform the ceremony, and the other three need to be there. Afterward, he wants to discuss Jade."

Venus pushed into the kitchen behind Deacon. "I'm surprised you had time to call after all that morning sex."

My cheeks burned. I'd never get used to others knowing what I did with Deacon behind closed doors. We had been quiet. I didn't think Dad knew. Avril hadn't acted differently around me before she left, but embarrassment flushed my body that everyone else did.

"You'll need to go too," Deacon said to Venus.

Tension rippled over Venus's body. Her expression turned to stone. "Fair. I might need a stiff drink to face this mess."

Steel's brows drew together. "I'm all for ASAP, but we still have a little time. Is he afraid it'll fall through?"

A memory sifted through my brain.

Deacon answered his brother. "He wants to make sure everything is wrapped up before Venus's brother learns of it."

Penn's concerned gaze was on Venus. Steel watched his brother. His words *we still have a little time* echoed through my head.

Deacon needed to be mated before his thirty-fifth birthday.

We still have a little time.

"When is your birthday?" My words came out quiet.

No one moved in the kitchen.

"Three days," Deacon said softly. "My birthday is on Friday."

My oath. The pressure. How Deacon said all the right things. He did all the right things.

Because he was in a rush. Because he didn't want to marry Venus, a strong, defiant woman. He wanted to marry a meek, compliant girl. And he had to do it before Friday.

And just like I did with Chance, I accommodated Deacon. I was willing to change my entire life, and leave my family once again, for a man.

Deacon was no ordinary man, but that didn't matter. He was just like the rest of them when it really mattered.

"I'm so stupid," I whispered.

"Ava—"

I stood and sliced a hand through the air. "I don't want to hear it."

"What do you mean?"

I shook my head. "You knew exactly what to do. And I fell for it." Tears welled in my eyes and spilled onto my cheeks. "I fell for all of it."

TWENTY

eacon

Ava rushed out of the kitchen toward the guest room.

I charged after her. "It's not what you think."

She already had her duffel bag open on the bed and was charging around the room, gathering her things. "Oh, yeah? You don't have to find a mate by Friday? You really do want to marry Venus? You don't want a quiet little human mate who has no power against you?"

"What are you talking about? I'm not looking for someone subservient. We have a connection."

She couldn't deny it. She was drawn to me. I had made sure of it. "The connection that means I have to leave my dad, and I have to find a new job, and I have to move to a new town, and I have to do whatever you want me to. Until you decide you don't want me anymore."

"Our vows are concrete. They're eternal."

"Too bad they aren't truthful."

She dumped her items in her duffel bag and yanked the zipper shut. I was standing in the doorway, but when she stomped toward me, I moved. She wasn't my prisoner.

"I want to be with you, Ava. I haven't lied about a thing."

"You can't lie about what you don't say." She stormed down the hall. "And you sure as hell omitted some important details."

We passed a wide-eyed Venus and my brothers, each with an expression of growing alarm.

"Dad!" Ava flew down the stairs. "I'm going home with you. I'll be out in the pickup."

And she was out the door. By the time I reached the landing, Dorian was coming up the stairs, his overnight bag in his hand.

His gaze swiveled from me to the screen door. "Is everything all right?"

"No," I growled. I shoved a hand through my hair, wanting to go after Ava, but not wanting to worry her dad more than he was. "That ex of hers poisoned her thinking. She doesn't think I'm serious about her."

Dorian nodded, understanding and sympathy filling his eyes. "Give her time. She'll come around."

Exactly the problem. I didn't have time.

Dorian scooted past me to push out the door. I was about to follow when he stopped and faced me. "You need to give her some space. I heard the yelling. Her emotions are still hot, and she's been hurt pretty bad. This last week has gone pretty fast between you two."

"I really need to talk to her."

Dorian's tone was fatherly but firm. "If you're

wanting to talk to her in order to get your way, then you need to rethink what you're going to say. You need time too." He dipped his head. "I can't thank you enough for your hospitality, but you've got to let her go. And if this is real, she'll be back."

If only he knew how dire the circumstances were. But I couldn't get beyond what he said. I did only want to talk to Ava to get my way. I didn't want her to leave. She was my mate, I could feel it. I had fallen for her as soon as I had seen her. And over the last week, I just tumbled further and further. But there was a deadline over my head. And the consequence of her oath over hers. Whether or not I liked it, that changed things.

Steel appeared at the top of the stairs. "Fuck, they're pulling away. Go after her."

I shook my head. "No."

Penn appeared next to Steel. "You want her to die?"

I let out a long exhale.

Venus stood behind Penn. She pressed her hands to her stomach like she was holding back a wave of sickness. "Are we going to have to mate?"

Penn's jaw clenched. Steel was nodding when I said, "No. I'm not going to be with anyone but Ava."

Steel threw his arm out, gesturing at the driveway. "Then you'd better go fucking get her."

I wouldn't do that. "Load up. We'll all go face the council together."

Steel dropped his arm. Grim resignation rested in his eyes. He knew what decision I had made. He may not be the leader of the clan, but it was still his duty as one of the ruling families to know all the rules.

Penn read the heavy air between us and came to the

same conclusion. "No. You can't." He shoved his hands through his hair. "Fuck, Deacon. *You can't.*"

"I can, and I will. Let's go talk to the council."

~

AVA

I FINISHED SOBBING by the time Dad drove through Bottineau. I hadn't been able to appreciate any of the scenery. Not the trees. Or the cows and horses in the pastures. I thought about how perfect Deacon seemed until he wasn't. He turned out to be the guy I initially met, and I'd had such an easy time romanticizing him.

"It'll be okay, kiddo." Dad pulled into a gas station and stopped at a gas pump, but he hadn't gotten out yet. "I really think you two had something, and you'll work it out."

"I thought so too. But I was just convenient."

He gave me a sidelong look. "Venus was convenient. They would've made it work if he was that desperate to get married."

"I won't give the resistance she would."

"Oh, Ava. You gave him resistance." He went to open his door but stopped. "I just don't get why a guy his age would need an arranged marriage."

I shrugged and gave him a look that said, *What can you do?* I had explained it as a promise Deacon had made to his dad before he died. That his dad had been afraid he would wrap himself up in work and grow old alone. Dad bought it, but I wished I could tell him the truth. Lying to him was just pouring salt all over my wounds.

Dad finally got out to fill the pickup with gas. I couldn't stand to be alone with my thoughts. I slid out of the cab and wandered into the gas station.

I should be hungry. I missed breakfast, and I hadn't eaten since the previous evening. But I couldn't stomach looking at any of the food. It was packaged to be appealing and that was the last thing I wanted to be surrounded by. A bunch of junk food with due dates. To be used by a date. It was a convenience store, and I was conveniently going to buy their food before they had to destroy it. The situation sounded familiar.

Okay, so I was looking into my surroundings a little too hard. I stayed outside and went to the edge of the building. Dad was still gassing up. Each set of pumps had at least one car. People coming and going about their days. People who didn't seem shattered.

A sporty red Mercury whipped into the parking lot.

I frowned as I watched it. There was no way Venus could be here. She stopped her car in a place that wasn't a parking spot and blocked the pathway for moving traffic. She got out and charged toward me. I didn't know what to do, so I stood there.

"Do you know what's going to happen?" Venus asked, her voice so low I could barely hear it. I frowned and looked around. She hadn't gotten many glances other than being a six-foot blonde charging a shorter woman.

"You're going to have to be with him?" My heart broke as I said it. I didn't want anyone else to be with Deacon. But maybe what she could have with him would be more real than what I thought we had.

"No." Venus's voice shook. "He's refusing to consider anyone else. He's ready to give up his life."

"Why would he have to give up his life? I get his birthday is soon, but he's mentally sound. He has time."

Venus shook her head and stepped closer, towering over me. "Not when you're the leader of the Silver clan. None of the leaders get a pass on the thirty-fifth birthday. They are the example to the rest of us. They are to show us that if we don't follow the rules, we will be terminated."

Terminated? "They're going to kill him?"

"Yeah," Venus said, like she couldn't believe I had to clarify.

I didn't want Deacon to die. Rage was mushroom clouding inside of me. How could he let them do that? How could the council do it? No, this wasn't my problem. Deacon's birthday wasn't until Friday.

"Well, he has some time."

A guy like him should be able to find someone else in two days. Was there anyone as gullible as me around Silver Lake?

Venus slammed her hands into her hips. "No, he doesn't. Because you made an oath and broke it. He's taking your punishment."

"What punishment?" I'd been around dragon shifters for days. I knew shifters like Deacon doled out punishments. But they would've punished me? Because I didn't keep my word and I left?

"When we make a vow, we keep it. To break our word means to lose our life. It's the grounds our society is built on. In this modern day and age, if we can't keep our word, we can't be trusted with our secrets. Oath breakers leave too much to chance."

I had to let that sink in for a moment. I swore myself

to Deacon. Then I broke up with him. I would've been killed, but now he was going to die?

"I don't understand."

"The council knew you made an oath. And Deacon's not showing up with you to mate. So instead of the council sending him or his brothers after you, he's relinquishing his life." Fear rippled through Venus's expression. "Look, I have my reasons for why I don't want to mate Deacon. But none of those matter when it comes to my clan. I was willing to take my out when you showed up, but that was because I had the leader of Silver clan on my side. When he's gone, I don't know what Lachlan's going to do with me. I might be treated like another trading card."

"That isn't fair." The rage that was directed toward the threat to Deacon's life was now anger about everything. "All I wanted was a vacation with my dad, and I ended up trading my life for his. Don't get me wrong, I'd do it again." Would I? Would I have issues if someone other than Deacon had demanded an oath? "But in the end, he's just another guy who uses me as he sees fit."

Venus relaxed slightly. She folded her arms across her chest, a stance that looked less hostile than before. "I get it, Ava. I really do. But he's not your ex. He went to a lot of lengths to protect you from the oath."

She held up a hand as I opened my mouth.

"I know he forced you to make it. But you've been so wrapped up in the past, ready to let that ex of yours dictate your future, that I don't think you saw everything Deacon did for you that he didn't have to. Because the honest truth is, if he didn't care, you'd be dead and I'd be moving my things into his cabin. You're running out of time. So now that you have all the information, make your decision—and be damn sure you can live with it."

Dad approached me. "Is everything okay here?"

I couldn't answer him at first. Nothing was okay. Venus's words ricocheted through my head. *Be damn sure you can live with it.*

Deacon was taking the punishment for me. And according to Venus, even if he didn't, he would be executed anyway. Because he wasn't going to be with anyone else.

He didn't have to protect me. He had options. He could choose someone else. He was choosing to lose his life instead, and he was choosing to save mine.

I was nothing to him right now. I had broken my oath. I had refused to mate him. Yet he was willing to undo everything he did and let me go at great cost to himself. He was ready to pay everything.

I pressed my fingers to my temples. "Dad, I think I made a mistake."

TWENTY-ONE

Deacon

"DAMMIT, DEACON. DON'T DO THIS." Orla's voice shook.

She was the oldest council member and she'd never looked frailer. Each member of the council was shaken. Their job was to make the tough calls for our clan and for our people overall. This would be one of their hardest, and it was my fault. I could've prevented it, but I didn't know how. With the deadline hanging over my head, the outcome might've been the same.

My brothers didn't question me. They knew I'd made my decision, and they knew I wouldn't sacrifice Ava to save a few days. I didn't hold a grudge against her. I loved her and I'd failed her. No one else saw it the same way, but that was what happened.

"We can hunt her down," Simon said as he paced the meeting room.

"It's my right to make the trade. It's now, or on Friday."

Deborah's lips were thin and she kept glancing at me, then looking away, her eyes glittering with unshed tears. "We haven't lost a leader like this in centuries."

We hadn't. Other shifters would make a business arrangement. They'd mate and they'd live on. Maybe they fell in love, maybe they didn't. Maybe they procreated, maybe they didn't. But they didn't let go of the one they loved. They didn't have to do this to save her life. I did, and I would do it again a thousand times.

"I have a request," I said.

Bronson let out a disgusted noise. "Haven't you done enough?" His pain was evident.

The council frustrated the shit out of me. They weren't exactly friends, and they weren't family. But they were my council. I respected their advice, their experience, and their insight. They were important to me, and I was important to them.

They would lead Steel through assuming my mantle. Between them and my brothers, they'd handle Jade clan.

It'd be fine.

Everything would be fine.

My throat grew thick. "I'd like to be at home when Steel carries out his duty."

"Fuck," Steel gritted out. "Just... fuck."

Bronson's Adam's apple bobbed up and down like he couldn't get words beyond his throat. The council exchanged looks with each other, and Orla nodded.

"We can accommodate. But understand that we will have to escort you there, not your brother."

To make sure I didn't shirk my duty. To make sure my brothers didn't abduct me against my will and hide me until an impossible miracle happened. They'd accompany me to my final resting place, and then they'd confirm that Steel carried out the first task of his new position.

Penn slapped a heavy hand on my shoulder.

I dipped my head and walked out of the meeting room. Outside, I tipped my head to the sky and let the fresh breeze caress my face. I wouldn't delay, but neither would I rush to my death. I wanted to savor nature. I wanted a few extra minutes to apologize to Steel and Penn. And I wanted time to remember Ava. I wanted to remember the euphoria of planning my mating ceremony.

My brothers got into my pickup. Steel was in the driver's seat. The vehicle was his now. Everything that was mine would be his and Penn's. Steel didn't start the pickup. He was like me and wouldn't be rushing a thing.

"Come along," Orla said quietly. She put her hand on my shoulder and left it there a few heartbeats longer than she normally would've. "Dammit, I'll miss you."

"Likewise." I patted her soft fingers.

She'd witnessed a lot of tragedy in her time. I hated to add more, but she would help the others move on.

She chuffed softly. "You won't be around to miss us. You're the fortunate one in this scenario. And you're human."

"I hope you understand."

"Humans don't know the weight of our obligations." She gave me a disgruntled but knowing look. "And I doubt you told her."

I gave her a small smile. "I didn't."

"You wouldn't place a burden that heavy on some-one's shoulders. It's what made you a good leader."

"Steel will be a strong replacement."

She leaned in close. "But he'll be broken, Deacon." She shuffled away, leaving me feeling like I'd chosen Ava's life over my brother's.

Which I had, in a way.

I went to Bronson's car. I took one last look at city hall. My family had served here for generations. They'd built this place. All of it. From the ground up. The Silvers had left the caves and formed Silver Lake and made a good life for our people among the humans.

I opened the door. My last ride under Bronson's watchful eye.

Tires squealed at the corner. Venus's car sped down the street.

And she wasn't alone. She'd barely stopped the car when Ava hopped out. She ran around the front of the Mercury, half sliding over the hood, her golden hair glowing under the sun.

"Deacon!"

I left the door hanging open and met her in the street. "Ava?"

She propelled herself into my arms. "Don't you dare. Don't you dare let them touch you."

I hugged her to me. I couldn't bring myself to believe she had a change of heart. I knew she didn't want me to die, but I'd break my own neck right here to keep her from offering herself up.

"Is it too late?" she asked.

"You're not turning yourself in. I won't hurt you, and I won't let anyone else."

She placed her hands on either side of my face. "No, to be with you?"

My sluggish mind had a hard time keeping up. She'd left me and my brain hadn't accepted that she was here.

"When Steel executes me?"

Venus appeared next to us and smacked my shoulder. "To mate you, dumbass. I didn't break twenty driving laws to bring her back as a witness."

My brothers stood behind her and the council surrounded us.

Ava came back to save me. My heart soared, then stalled. It didn't change anything. It made it harder. I stared into Ava's wide green eyes.

"I'm not letting you give up your life for me. I tricked you. I made all kinds of excuses, but that's the root of what happened. I forced you, and then I made it seem like it was your decision, but I didn't tell you everything for a reason."

"Yes, you did, but I'm having a really hard time caring right now." She rested her hands on my shoulders. "I wouldn't be giving up anything. I'd be gaining a partner who's willing to risk everything for me. A person who makes me feel like a treasure. A guy who cared so much about me that he omitted several details and worked diligently to get me to fall in love with him. And it worked, by the way."

"Ava." Was it true? I didn't sense a lie. I sensed only desperation and honesty. "Because I've loved you since I first saw you."

"I tried so hard not to. I still can't believe someone like you would be interested in me, but I'm willing to take the chance."

"Ava Payne, will you be mine?"

She stood on her tiptoes and said loud enough for everyone to hear, "I swear it."

Bronson cleared his throat. "This is great news. Great.

And I hate to be a downer, but before we carry out the ceremony, what are we going to do about Jade clan?"

Venus blanched. "I'll handle my clan."

Penn stepped forward, his gaze on Venus. "Tell them I'm taking my brother's place."

Venus made a choking sound. "What? No."

The council exchanged glances in the way I'd known them to do.

Orla spoke. "Your brother may find Steel the better option. He's second-in-command."

"But I didn't offer. Penn did." Steel's voice was gruff, like he was trying to hide the panic growing in his expression.

I didn't want to take my eyes off Ava. "I'll contact them when the ceremony is over. I can see if Penn is a suitable option, but I'm not going to be the one forcing Venus into anything." I owed her my life.

"I'm not a jewel to get passed around," Venus sputtered.

"This will buy you time." As much as I agreed with her, she had almost a month until her birthday and Penn's offer might mollify her clan until then. "I'm confident you'll work something out. But this will buy you time."

Penn shoved his hands into his pockets, his expression mixed parts determined and crestfallen. "Or you can just mate me."

Venus barely spared him a glance. "You're a baby."

"You'll find I'm no such thing," he growled.

Venus's cheeks tinted pink, but I intervened before she said something she'd regret. Whether she liked it or not, Penn was saving her ass right now. "You can stay in

Silver Lake as long as you need. I'll deal with your brother."

She clenched her jaw. Her gaze brushed over Penn before quickly darting away. Was she drawn to him?

"I've stayed long enough. I'll deal with Lachlan." She pivoted to go back to her car.

"Venus." Ava rushed to her and swung her arms around the taller female. She wasn't enough to knock Venus off balance.

Venus didn't return the hug, but the poleaxed look on her face told me it was shock freezing her in place.

"Thank you, and I'm sorry. I wish there was something I could do."

Vulnerability touched Venus's green eyes and it probably killed her to let us see it. Shifters of Jade clan weren't the apologizing type. I couldn't imagine how Ava's reaction affected her.

"I'm a big girl. I can handle it." She finally wrapped her arms around Ava's shoulders and gave her a squeeze. "Congratulations. I'm really glad it worked out."

"It will for you too," Ava whispered.

Venus kept her back to Penn as she released Ava. "Let me talk to my brother first."

"Let me know when you do. I'll help you any way I can." That was a promise I wasn't afraid to make.

When Venus drove away, I tucked Ava back into my side. A grin spread across my face. "Time to make Ava mine."

∼

"I don't need a ceremony," Ava said as she swung on the porch swing next to me. "I told Dad we eloped and he was fine with it."

"What about a celebration?" I didn't want her to look back on this time and think she missed out. I'd had my brothers and the council. Ava had been by herself.

"Maybe next summer, so Avril doesn't have to make another trip." She laid her head on my shoulder. "I'm fine, Deacon. I really am. But I'm not too proud to admit I can't wait for my ring to be finished."

The princess cut ruby in a silver setting. I couldn't wait to see my stone on her hand. "Are you going to wear your mother's ring too?"

She feathered her fingers over the area my teeth had been under the collar of her shirt. As soon as our vows had been uttered, I'd dismissed everyone and claimed her.

A smile played over her lips as if she was remembering the moment I'd made her mine. "I thought about that. Maybe it'll be the start of my own hoard."

I laughed, delighted to have a human mate who readily accepted my kind and our ways.

She twined her fingers through mine. "Happy Birthday."

"It's the best one yet."

She chuckled. "We haven't done anything."

Oh, we'd done plenty. For the first time since I'd met her—which wasn't that long ago but still—I had her and the house to myself. We'd spent most of the morning in bed. Then we ate brunch on the patio while the birds chirped around us.

We'd just returned from a hike to the creek. She'd

wanted to see my dragon, and we put the big rock to good use.

"Nope, we haven't done a thing, and it's perfect. All my adult life, my birthdays were nothing but countdowns. Venus and I put off fulfilling our contract for years. Each birthday, I was afraid she would change her mind and want to get it over with."

"She probably felt the same."

"I hope she figures something out."

"I hope she figures out that your brother is a pretty good option."

I playfully nudged her. "What are you saying?"

She lifted her head and grinned. "Other than being partial to Silver men—males—I think he adores her. And I really hope the feeling is mutual, and it's just the age that's getting to her."

"Would you have an issue mating someone ten years younger than you?"

She laughed. "The whole world would. He'd be fifteen. But if I was Venus's age and you were twenty-five? I don't know."

"You're ten years younger than me."

"It's different for women. Females." She sighed. "That's going to take some getting used to. Anyway, it's different. And I imagine since your kind is all alpha and bloodlines and strength, it looks like she's weak and can't find a mate herself to bail out of the impending thirty-fifth birthday execution."

I could see that. Venus was a proud shifter. She'd been isolated because of her clan's reputation, and I'd never heard her people say a good thing about her. They didn't think highly of her and the longer I was around her, the more I didn't understand why. And now she'd gone from being the one to help unite our clans to being passed around like none of us wanted her.

Except Penn wanted her. I knew that now.

I owed Venus a favor. I owed her nearly everything. Mating Ava put her at risk. Did Venus really not feel anything for my brother? Was it too simple of a solution that it was wrong?

I didn't know. The questions dimmed the happy afterglow of my mating.

I wrapped my arm around Ava. I wasn't wrong to hope for a love like this for my brothers and Venus too. Hell, even Venus's brother Lachlan and his mate. A happy mating might mellow his attitude. Or at least keep him restricted to his bedroom for a while. Because that was all I wanted to do with Ava every damn day.

"I'd like to look for a job," she said.

"You don't need my approval."

"Thanks for the reassurance," she said wryly.

She could get anything she wanted, but she'd never need my permission.

"I might need your advice. I went to school for accounting but I never followed up on it. I took the first job I was offered and it was selling life insurance, but I'd like to do what I went to school for."

"Open your own office."

"No, I couldn't. I'm not a CPA."

"Can't you be one?"

"I guess. I've been out of school for a few years, and I don't have any experience, so..."

"Ava, you can do anything you want. You aren't restricted to being my mate. If you want to be a CPA, you have my full support. If you want to find a small family business to do the books for, you have my full support. If you want to retire and stay in my bed, I might not get a lot of my work done, but you have my support."

"I want a job that will let me be flexible." She bit her lower lip. "For when we have kids."

"Oh, yeah?" My grin had to be predatory. The image of her belly rounded with my young called to everything primal inside of me. "You plan to have a few kids?"

"I don't know," she said, looking up at me through her lashes. "What are you planning?"

"Whatever you let me get away with."

When she laughed, the sunlight made her hair glitter like spun gold. "How about we start with one? Give me a few months and then we can start trying."

"Okay, but I'm going to need a lot of practice."

She poked me in the side. "Your brothers are going to be here soon."

They were coming for a birthday grill out. It didn't start for an hour. I gathered her in my arms and rose.

"Then we'd better hurry."

———

VENUS MIGHT BE A DRAGON SHIFTER, but can she get over feeling like a cougar when Penn pursues her in The Dragon's Promise?

WANT a bonus epilogue with Deacon and Ava and another (new) member of the family? You can download it here.

About the Author

Marie Johnston writes paranormal and contemporary romance and has collected several awards in both genres. Before she was a writer, she was a microbiologist. Depending on the situation, she can be oddly unconcerned about germs or weirdly phobic. She's also a licensed medical technician and has worked as a public health microbiologist and as a lab tech in hospital and clinic labs. Marie's been a volunteer EMT, a college instructor, a security guard, a phlebotomist, a hotel clerk, and a coffee pourer in a bingo hall. All fodder for a writer!! She has four kids, an old cat, and a puppy that's bigger than half her kids.

mariejohnstonwriter.com

Follow me:

Also by Marie Johnston

Silver Dragon Shifter Brothers

The Dragon's Oath

The Dragon's Promise

The Dragon's Vow

Jade Dragon Shifter Brothers

The Dragon's Pledge

Want to try my very first shifter series?

<u>The Sigma Menace</u>

Fever Claim (Book 1)

Primal Claim (Book 2)

True Claim (Book 3)

Reclaim (Book 3.5)

Lawful Claim (Book 4)

Pure Claim (Book 5)